DAWNBREAK

The Farthest Star Series - Book 1

By Rebecca Mickley

Edited By: Kat Luck

Copyright © 2018 by Rebecca Mickley
1st Edition Print published by
Rebecca Mickley and Studio Prey, 2019

Content Editing by Kathrine Luck
Line Editing by Speedy876

Cover Illustration by Sara Coty
Copyright © 2018 by Studio Prey
Book design and production by Studio Prey

Beta Reading by the Studio Prey Final Draft Club
with Special Thanks to:
Maya Sora
Kayla Dowdy

E-mail the author at snowy@studioprey.com

Visit the author's website at
www.studioprey.com

First Printing, June 2019
Studio Prey

First Edition

ISBN: 978-1-951066-00-0

Other Titles By Rebecca Mickley

The Farthest Star Series

Available on StudioPrey.com
Gateways – Book 0.5 (Only available on StudioPrey.com)
Dawnbreak – Book 1
Exile's Return – Book 2
Rise of the Forgotten – Book 3
The Farthest Star – Book 4
Sins of the Solar Republic – Book 5
Electronic Souls – Book 6
Captain Tosk – Book 7
Starfall – Book 8
Angels of Our Yesterday – Book 9
Demons of Our Tomorrow – Book 10

The Nightmare God Series

Hillsong Chronicles Series

Acknowledgements

There are a myriad of people that have gone to great lengths to see this book to completion, and published.

I would be remiss if I did not begin such an entry without acknowledging Kat the Dragon, Britt Luck, Page Shepard, Maya Sora, Waggs, Sarah Coty and Kayla Dowdy. These committed souls have devoted untold hours to the success of this work.

In addition to these fine souls, I'd like to thank all of my Patreon supporters and members of the Final Draft Club. Thank you for everything you've done to make the magic happen.

Finally I would like to acknowledge all of my friends and family that have stood by and encouraged me to believe in myself and my dreams. I love you all, and would be nowhere without you.

Onward, towards the Farthest Star...

Studio
Prey

Rebecca
Mickley

Katharine Luck

Britt Luck

Page Shepard

Sara Coty

CONTENTS

For my Husband, the author of my hope. None of these works would exist without you. We will make it to the Farthest Star ...together. I love you with all of me.
—Rebecca Mickley

Chapter 1

When I was growing up, most other girls wanted a pony, but not me.

I wanted to *be* a sea otter.

It was a fantasy, a hope; a secret inner identity that I quickly learned, through the blood sport cruelty of childhood social existence, to keep to myself, my daydreams and my drawings.

My identity calcified around that one fact, and so I quietly grew apart. I wanted to be a sea otter, but to my mind and my heart, I already was; I was just stuck living a human experience.

It was my deepest truth, my most hidden belief. How could anyone understand something so alien, so different, as not identifying with the species you were born with?

And so I hid. Hiding became a way of life, and I soon became addicted to its convenience. There was no reason to reach out, no reason to share that hidden part of myself and risk the pain, until suddenly, there was.

I was in the nursing program at Ohio State University, but was doing a summer internship at Jerusalem Fleet Academy. The Earth military was actively recruiting, and it was one of a few ways to pay for college.

The program was a bust; I found out I was unfit for military life, but elected to tough it out; a summer in Jerusalem, even with inspections, was infinitely better than Columbus, Ohio.

Still, the summer dragged on; moments of freedom punctuated by long periods of ritual and military routine, until the fateful day when I met John Dawkins.

We had been paired up on a blind date together and got to talking. One thing led to another, and then, there was something, besides avoiding Columbus, that had me wanting to stay in Jerusalem.

Heady first love, the passionate quest to share everything, to learn about each other. I dared, in a fit of utter disastrous foolishness, to share my secret, though I had bore the scars of failed attempts from so many times before.

I liked him, desperately, and so I wanted him to know me.

A fateful connection. I shared my secret, and then he… shared his.

A lifetime of difference, a lifetime of being alone, but we had found each other, an otter and a hare.

The romance faded as summertime loves do, but our friendship remained, forged in the impossible truth that we were somehow the same. We became inseparable in spite of the distance, and now, he had returned with hope itself; hope in tangible form.

"Joyce?" John inquired, snapping me out of my reflection.

"Sorry, was thinking of past things. When was the last time you heard from Sandy?" I asked, my curiosity piqued by my brief walk in nostalgia.

"Oh years now, she graduated that summer and I think is at Lunar One now. Haven't really had the time to keep up," he shrugged. The answer didn't surprise me. After her attempts at matchmaking produced a disappointing friendship, she seemed to fade from our lives, moving on quickly to her next project.

"You know there are more layoffs coming at the hospital next quarter," I mentioned, pivoting the conversation. Fewer people were dying as nanitic treatments revolutionized medicine and extended the life span. Gerontology and "Nanitic Maintenance" were the only growing fields these days, and with the news of the Treaty of Gates and Morphic Tech, I had lost all interest.

"Please. Can we wait to have this conversation again? I just got in from the dock, I'm tired. Press hasn't left me alone," he complained, definitely having seen it coming.

"I don't understand how you can be like that. I don't understand how you can be this calm. It's possible dammit. Why would you want to wait?" I pushed.

"Your field is experiencing layoffs so you are going to throw all caution to the wind, become a sea otter and live on an alien planet?" he asked, his tone incredulous.

"It's cruel when you put it that way, Hoppy," I spat. He narrowed his eyes at me, sighing. The fight was on. We were both caught in its gravity.

"I'm thrilled about Shift Tech, but I'm suspicious too. They aren't opening the Gates to anything but probes until it's publicly released. Why would anyone do that? It makes no sense, unless they want something. It scares me, Joyce. Let someone else be the first, let someone else take that risk. I've got two years left on my contract. By then it will be well understood; we can go through the process together, and then go from there. What's the rush?" he said.

"Did those space snakes replace you with a copy or something? Are you hearing yourself? Why rush? We've both been rushing towards this our whole lives. It feels like fate, John. You can leverage your position on the First Contact team, to get them to let you out early to shift. The Mendians would love that and you know it. Then we can leave this all behind and be part of something real; start a colony together. The Morphic Colony Committee even selected a planet today, Centioc One."

"You know what we are calling it in the service? The shift and fuck off club. It's a risk," he insisted.

14

"And it's worth it. I'm tired of waiting John, I'm tired of hurting all the damn time. How can you ask me to wait when there's an answer? All I had to do was sign up for the colony and I'm in the first five-hundred. There's still space. You don't have to wait," I begged. It seemed cruel to leave him behind. Deny all he wanted, I knew this was his dream as much as it was mine.

"No," he said flatly, finishing his beer before rising. "You do what you want. You're my best friend and I'll support you, but at the very least, I'm finishing out my contract and seeing where this goes. I'm in no rush to become somebody's puppet, or worse. There are just too many questions right now," he replied.

Chapter 2

I was running late.

Shift change report had run long at work, mainly because my relief had been late and now I was scrambling.

The Morphic Colony Committee was meeting today, and voting on a starship; that was the official reason. We had to select one that we would buy from the UEA that was, up to now floating in a boneyard. The unofficial reason was why I was stopping by the liquor store on the way despite being late.

It was early September; the Shift Tech Beta Program had been approved and we were all in.

Tonight we would pick our colony ship and celebrate.

A strange man in a black jacket appeared to have been watching me from a distance as I loaded the bottles into the back of my car. Gripping my keys tightly in my left hand, I quickly made my way to the relative safety of the cabin of my vehicle.

With one eye behind me and one on the door, a quick sense of panic built as I fumbled with my keys; a growing worry that he might be behind me, that I might not be quick enough.

Sliding in and locking the doors, my sense of safety returned as I drifted away and quickly forgot about the creepy guy. Today was a day to celebrate. In two short months, I would be at United Earth Medical getting my first boosters, the start of the process.

Checking the clock on the dash, I was already a half hour late, with more than ten minutes to go. *Damn.* I sped up, bending the traffic laws.

It did little good, but it helped my morale at least.

Crossing Woz Way, I soon slid into a small, disused building parking lot; it was an old church-turned-community center, so it still retained it's sacred appearance.

Crossing the threshold, I arrived just as the vote ended. We had a ship and I had missed it.

"What did we get?" I asked Ricky, as he turned to welcome me. The crowd was breaking up, as the official business was over.

"An ancient Gen 1 cruiser, the *Horn Shark*. BEC Fusion Drive Gen 1; thing is practically an antique," he laughed. Ricky was our chief engineer and a future ocelot.

"Can you make it work?" I asked, and a look of feigned shock appeared on his face.

"You dare question my prowess? I'm not just an engineer, I'm a legacy." He struck a dramatic pose, as I mouthed the words along with him.

"Grew up around the BEC-1's. No problem. They aren't too temperamental," he confirmed, full of optimism.

17

"Problems?" Sonya poked her head out from the former sanctuary.

"No problems Sonya, just getting caught up," I replied.

"Well how about the other way? You're late ya know," she reminded me. I hadn't forgotten.

"The report sometimes runs long, and I had to stop by the liquor store for the party, you know how it goes," I shrugged.

"So why didn't we pick a newer ship?" I pushed, it seemed silly. The colony was being underwritten by a grant from the UEA and Martian Marauder Incorporated.

"Oh, another program the UEA wants us to trial. In exchange for taking the older vessel, we get a newer auto freighter that we can deorbit and turn into housing. It works out," Ricky reported.

"Makes sense. We're already guinea pigs in so many ways, might as well double down," I commented.

"You never know, there may be one aboard the ship," Sonya replied

"Wasn't that Kevin?" I mentioned.

"It's kangaroo rat you sea-loving asshole," yelled a voice with a New England accent from where the altar once stood.

We all shared a laugh as Kevin slid over to join us.

"Hey freaks," he said casually, holding a drink in his left hand.

"Says the one that grew up at the edge of the Zone," I teased.

"You calling me a mutant? That old game. What, should I call you a hippy?" Boston was on the edge of the habitable zone. A nuclear exchange had wiped out New York and Washington D.C in 2030.

"Nah, we won't be mutants for a few more months," Ricky chimed in, not content to simply watch the banter.

"Fair," he replied.

"So we're doing this?" I volunteered. "Moving to a new planet?"

Another figure walked up to the growing party. I may have missed the vote, but there was still plenty to do and discuss.

We had a ship, and were moving to an alien planet. There was a lot to talk about.

A tall and imposing figure stepped up; he was easily 6'4, and well over three-hundred pounds. A giant of a man.

"Everybody getting to know each other then. I'm Mack, Mack Douglas." He spoke with a British accent, which gave the impression of a cultured, gentle giant.

"Oh hi! Yeah we spoke by tablet a few days ago. I'm Joyce Coswell, the medic for the colony." I offered my hand, slipping into professional habits.

"Colony coordinator, as you well know. Boot strapping up with Ricky here, good Lad," Mack continued, as he made a gesture, to which Ricky humbly smiled.

"I just keep the mechanics running. Paperwork is your monster, man," Ricky responded.

"Been that way since college. I talk it up, you make it look good," Mack replied. It was clear they were old friends.

"If this shift works out how we're expecting, you're the one who'll be looking good." Ricky said, as Mack blushed.

I looked at them both, my curiosity building.

"I uh." Mack said.

"How's the family business?" Ricky asked with a grin, throwing Mack a lifeline.

"Oh, Dad is still trying to talk me into it. Bloody disappointed with the news as of late." He looked down at his massive hands, as if looking for something.

"You're wasted running a logistics company. Mars will always find a way to get its fruit. This is starting a new world," Ricky volunteered.

"I hear you. Looking forward to building something of my own, not have it just handed to me. Blood and sweat. Something real. Something true." He drifted off.

"Now that's a recruiting poster," Kevin commented, and we all shared the laugh.

"Here, come outside and help me unload," I offered.

We wandered out and started unloading bottles from the car. For the briefest of moments, I thought I saw the man in the black jacket again, sitting in his car down the street, but that was impossible. It wasn't like he had followed me.

We got inside and started setting up to get the party underway.

It was our first real meeting. I was one of the transplants into the team, having no previous connection. A call for a medic had gone out, and my Bachelors in Nursing made me an attractive candidate. My friendship with John and namedropping him to Mack as part of the first contact team in the interview, had guaranteed my place.

There was so much to do, and we were at best, a skeleton crew. Sonya was our financial expert, while Kevin worked navigation and communication. Mack knew how to run the ship and Ricky knew how to keep it working in deep space.

Just like the pioneer days, we had all gathered to chase the dream of what might lie over the next horizon, and were determined to find out what, no matter the risks.

Two hundred and forty-three other brave souls had joined, and were waiting for their embarkment letters.

It was our job to make sure they had supplies and a ship on which to board; and in the meantime, become a new person.

No pressure.

Still, for the night, there was the party.

Playful banter. The beginnings of new bonds. An hour passed by and we were all beginning to get comfortable with one another.

Then suddenly, a Molotov flew through the window.

It exploded into fire nearby the pulpit; liquid flames danced across the floor in hellish choreography, as the room devolved into screams.

Then another burst through the window on the other side. Mack was screaming; he fell to the floor, rolling, as Ricky threw a jacket over him patting him down, extinguishing the flames.

The smoke became choking, thick and oily; still, the exits were clearly visible and open. In a panic, we all rushed outside.

Four men in black jackets and ski masks were waiting in the back of a truck.

"You freaks are selling out your own kind. You deserve to burn!", one yelled before the truck peeled out. As we all fell back from the attackers, they threw one last cocktail in our direction, but we were already too far away. It pooled out in a fiery circle as we heard sirens in the distance.

"Joyce, you need to help Mack! He's burned pretty bad," Ricky called out.

"I can't do too much, I've had a few drinks," I commented before rattling off first aid advice. Nodding, he carried it out, while I observed, protecting my nursing license.

Firemen quickly arrived on scene, along with paramedics, blessedly relieving me from my duties.

I had no one to call. John was away on some kind of official business and would be gone until next week.

Instead, I just waited, related what I could remember to the police and hid under the grey blanket the firemen offered me.

The next few hours passed in a strange blur, as my statement was taken three separate times. My head was now cleared, as I hadn't drank that much, but still, the entire experience had left me numb.

The police kept saying something about anti-morphic groups. I had honestly never even heard the term before.

Why would anyone care? Weren't we leaving?

In that moment, the time couldn't come soon enough. The world seemed alien and terrifying and the idea that someone would do such a thing just astounded me.

It was futile to consider. Humans had always found reasons to divide and hate, and it seemed they were now finding another one.

The desire to shift suddenly surged harder, feeling almost like an act of defense, living in defiance of the barbarism I saw in them.

Knowing what I did about sea otters, made that slightly funny. They too, could be vicious creatures. Maybe it was a fact of life that everything had a dark side. It's just that when that dark side has a certain level of intelligence, it makes Molotov cocktails or nuclear bombs.

Talk about scale. Kevin had grown up on the ruined edges of that scale's extremes.

Still, the Mendians had made it, hadn't they? Earth wasn't burning, and for all their mysteriousness, they wanted to share. Was their success the proof that the ultimate trend for humanity was more hopeful than I dared imagine in that moment? After all, John had said they hadn't had a war in almost two thousand years.

The image of Mack burning pushed any idea of 'enlightened humans' firmly out of my mind. He had been transported and was in critical condition. No one knew for sure if he would survive, or what this would do to the possibilities of his shift.

We hadn't even started, and we were already losing people. It wasn't supposed to be like this. This was the dream, what I had been waiting for my entire life; it wasn't supposed to be a nightmare. No... I wouldn't let it become a nightmare.

This was the dawn of my hope; it was always coldest the last hours before the dawn, and ours was coming, just two short months away. Then, we would have a chance to start again, away from all the crazy.

After what felt like an eternity, I was finally officially released and cleared to leave the scene. I ordered a transport and immediately set out for home.

I wanted nothing more than a hot shower, my bed, and out of this species.

Just two short months after a lifetime of waiting, and my wish would come true.

Chapter 3

A week had passed. The police had no leads.

"So they just tanked him early?" John asked, astounded.

"Yeah, the burns were to 90% of his body. Our medical technology couldn't fight all the infection, so, they figured, why not try it? He agreed. It's going to be eleven months in but he's already stabilized floating in there," I reported.

"Shit. So there's a cure for everything now," John whistled, leaning back in his chair.

"Practically. Everything's changing John," I commented.

"Isn't that kind of the point?" he replied, laughing to himself.

"Fair," I nodded in agreement.

"So if they just put him in a tank, why don't they just put everyone in the tank, from the start? I don't understand what Earth is doing and you've been to the workshop," John remarked.

"Mainly because it's not necessary. It's a long time to check out, and we all still have lives. Seven months asleep is better than ten. That's at least how they explained it to me; I dunno." There had to be a method to the madness somewhere, but from what I understood, it was currently elusive.

There was a knock on the door.

"Message ma'am. Certified Post, sign here," she snapped efficiently.

The mystery deepened. Quickly signing it, I tore the envelope open.

The document inside bore my hospital's letterhead; it began with the words:

"Notice of Layoff and Severance Package- J.Coswell"

"More Changes." I waggled the piece of paper in the air. "I'm terminated!"

Dramatically, I faked my death over the couch.

"You seem so broken up about it, too," John said.

"I was quitting in the next six months anyway, and I get severance, unemployment, etc. I'll be fine. It doesn't matter anymore," I replied.

"Still, are you sure that's a healthy way to look at it? You worked your butt off for that job," he pushed, then continued. "Feel something, throw a pie, or a fit; wave if you're in there."

"Yeah, and I can still do my job, on Centioc; in the meantime, don't you think I have enough going on?" I countered.

"Hey, it's your life," he answered, holding up his hands, retreating back to his room.

Pouring myself a bowl of cereal, one of my favorite comfort foods, I flopped down and turned on the screen in the living room, flipping towards the news.

"Will the princess marry Dirk Johnson? Tune in next week to The Drama Bloc," intoned a voice over the speaker. I rolled my eyes.

Firm pass.

Breaking News: More high level meetings with the First Contact Team today, as the now, historically long, debriefing continues. UEA and Central Command remain tight lipped on details, saying that for now, there is no visible threat from the Mendians in spite of their level of technology. More on that situation as it develops.

It seemed apparent to me that if the Mendians wanted us dead, we would be. There persisted in me a pragmatic belief in their benevolence.

And in other news, protests continue at the capital tonight surrounding the Treaty of Gates, calling it blackmail, demanding more time before the technology is released upon the public. The UEA official spokesperson stated that while they respect the rights of all citizens to protest, they stand behind the Treaty of Gates and its fulfillment.

I switched the screen to cartoons, something more informative and productive, and ate my cereal in brooding silence.

Watching the cartoon canary smack the hell out of the alley cat brightened my mood some. The poor dumb bastard always came back for more, but the canary just kept handing it out relentlessly.

For once, at least in the cartoon world, the little guy didn't have to take it. Maybe we could make it like that on Centioc.

Centioc- Where the little guy wins.

The thought warmed my heart in a way that only hope can. When it's in full bloom, no matter the season by date, its spring.

It inspired in me an idea.

John was right, I did need something to do.

Running to my bedroom, I grabbed my tablet off its charging pad and dashed back to the living room, putting in a call to Ricky and Sonya, inviting them over for lunch.

If I was going to Centioc, and had nothing better to do, I might as well use my time to help build the colony.

Two messages chimed in quickly. They were both unemployed, and were in a similar situation to my own.

Well, maybe Sonya. Ricky was "retired" after twenty years serving in the UEA military. He had started his career aboard ships like the ancient Gen 1, something he referred to as the "bailing wire, duct tape and pressure suit days".

He was only forty-three, but he talked like a man twenty years older. I guess that was life in the military.

Distantly, I thought of what John might be like in twenty years, but with Shift Tech, that was now impossible to tell.

I hoped happier. I hoped that for all of us.

Two months out before the initial boosters, and something was already changing. In that moment, thinking of the harshness I saw at times in Ricky, and was beginning to see in John, it was a viewpoint they had, where shared experiences from a martial culture shaped their perspective.

For John, it had inspired such a forethinking caution in him that he was willing to deny his own dreams, while I eagerly sought to redefine my relationship with happiness.

If he hadn't gone to Jerusalem Fleet Academy, he might be with me now going through the shifting process, but that would have meant we would have never met.

Could that have somehow been better? To meet at a time when we could have our happiness, before we had ever shared the pain of its absence?

The idea seemed foreign. In truth, happiness had always seemed foreign on some level.

I'm not talking, black-hole-on–a-windy-day emo kind of never happy. I'm talking about happiness as an alien, an unfamiliar concept in your greater world.

There's no hatred of the concept, no shunning of it. It's simply an impossible dream. No matter how good the day or joyous the time, there is a garish truth that hangs like a blood red moon in the sky, heralding the deep and sinister conceit of it all.

In this world, for all the time I came close to that feeling of happiness, it had always seemed hollow, never full, authentic or complete.

There was one exception, a day I'd never forget, April 23rd, 2071. The memory was, in my mind, perfect. The clouds parted, and for the first time, true happiness felt real. It was the day I learned escape was possible, and my dreams could come true. There was finally a way that I could be a sea otter.

True happiness, as if for the first time, feeling full, whole and complete; like sunshine, unabated, the first hints of spring after an interminably long winter.

There was a way out. It was coming. The prison sentence was ending and new, more complete happiness began to grow within me with each revelation about the technology.

In that moment, I could see how its lack, and the struggles that John and I shared forged our connection; one I would never have with Ricky or with Sonya, even if it was now taking us on two separate paths.

Nudging my reality, my tablet chirped and vibrated, as a sound flowed from the smart speakers positioned around the apartment.

Someone was at the door.

Ricky and Sonya had brought burgers, and they had come early.

I set my philosophy aside, and dug into a working lunch.

Chapter 4

It was late October. My living room table had become an office desk; piles of papers stacked like skyscrapers, rose into a city of discord and poorly organized notes.

Running a colony is a gigantic pain in the ass.

I was riding the manic edge of some high and terrible wave between extreme stress and joy as the days ticked down.

The mountains of forms, paperwork and UEA bureaucratic horseshit that had to be filled out and returned verged a Sisyphean maze, and gave me a firsthand lesson in why I had never ventured into hospital administration.

This paper chasing craziness was three steps past insane.

Still, that was not my greatest challenge. In spite of the rendered wood pulp apocalypse currently underway in my living room, the biggest challenge as of yet, was finding a new place to meet.

I had given up and had the last meeting here which had resulted in an angry note from my apartment manager affixed to my door, threatening eviction if I ever brought "extremist elements" into the community ever again.

Didn't I live here too? I had lived here for four years and always been me; what was so strange about not wanting to suffer, that they had to pin labels like that?

Just two weeks before the boosters, and it was clearer than ever that humans would never make sense to me.

Two weeks, and then the spiritual divide would begin to become a physical one as well.

Electric excitement strummed through my chest, leaving behind a pleasant burning, as it chased down my spine, radiating out into my fingers. I eagerly tapped the simulated buttons on my screen, dialing my next number.

The location was a pool hall, on a rougher side of town, but I was running out of options, and we needed a place before our holiday meeting. We would be in the initials throes of shifting in November.

"Graves Pool Hall," a gravely voice, originating somewhere far more easterly, erupted over the line.

"Hi, my name is Joyce Coswell; my organization is interested in renting your hall in December." I went through the same old preamble that I had gone through ten other times that morning, quickly signing a form while I had a moment to be distracted.

The only way to keep up on the paperwork monsters was through steady attack. Never let them rest.

"Tell me more miss; its two-hundred credits for the night; a one-hundred credit holiday fee comes out to three-hundred for December, that fair for you?" he asked.

It was fucking extortion, but I had few options.

"Fair," I lied.

"Ok let me just get this form here. What's the name of your group?" he asked. I took a deep breath, moment of truth.

"The Morphic Colony Committee," I announced, holding my breath, waiting.

"You mean that mixer stuff? Lady, you're crazy and I got insurance regs, don't need the creds that badly." The line clicked off.

God. Fucking. Dammit.

I thudded my head down heavily next to a stack of papers. They tumbled, scattering everywhere.

Thanks universe, kick a girl when she's down.

I closed my eyes and repeated my mantra, "Two weeks. Two weeks. Two weeks".

Graves Pool Hall went on my bad list, which meant nothing, considering I wouldn't even be on the planet in ten months. Still, bad list.

Asshole.

Amid the paperwork and the never-ending sea of forms that mercilessly continued to flow in, a yellow packet had arrived yesterday, laced with ideas.

It had some papers and welcome forms, but it also had a data chip. Sliding it into my tablet, it was basically a 101 of the shifting process.

My first month, according to the simulated trials, brought serious flu-like symptoms. That seemed infinitely more fun to deal with at the moment.

Idly, I flipped through the forms, letting them distract me from the frustration and failure of the morning. It was the map of my pilgrimage.

And I wasn't alone, I reminded myself. They were all counting on me to find a place for the Christmas party.

I dug back in and dialed the next number.

Second verse same as the first… and the third… and the fourth… and the fifth.

I had struck out in San Jose; it was time to cast a wider net.

.

I finally hit pay dirt in Santa Cruz.

"Morphic Colony Committee? I saw something about that on the news. Are you one of them?" the man asked; for once, his tone not angry.

"Yes, I'm the interim colony administrator." I had gotten this far before, I prepared myself for disappointment.

"But I mean, what are you going to be?" My hopes were rising, he was sounding ever more sympathetic.

"A sea otter," I volunteered, reluctantly. This level of openness about things so essential inspired a sudden and vulnerable awkwardness.

"Well ok then. I have the place available, and I can give it to you for fifty credits. One condition," he said.

"Fifty credits? That's a steal! Mister, are you sure? I mean it's a deal, but are you sure?" Light, sudden joyous light. No more phone calls. It was over!

Thank you universe, I'm sorry I ever said a mean thing about you.

Wait... My excitement had caused me to gloss over an important detail.

"What's the condition?" I asked, nervousness drawing my elation out to a ragged and harsh edge. My chest vibrated as anxiety surged.

"I want to know all about it, this is whizbang sci-fi stuff," he replied, and I relaxed. We had found an ally.

"Sir, what's your name again?"

"Steve, Steve Berkowitz," he reported.

"I would be happy to, but you must come to the party, you will be an honored guest," I said, trying to be diplomatic, all the while feeling a deep and sincere gratitude.

"Well gee, yeah, I'll be there... Get me the details," he replied.

Chapter 5

Staring up at the ceiling, I blinked my eyes. The sound of dripping was coming from a faucet in the kitchen.

There was no other sound. The apartment was quiet. It was the night before. Well, a few hours before, now.

I hadn't slept beyond small fits here and there for the last few days. My excitement was riding to fever pitch as the hours ticked by, as if suspended in some type of thick fluid.

The clock had become my most hated enemy. In a few hours I would be on my way to United Earth Medical to start the boosters.

The clock jumped forward an hour and a half when I wasn't looking as my eyes snapped open again, and immediately itched, feeling puffy from the fatigue.

Drip. Drip. Drip.

I had put in two maintenance requests about that damn faucet. Lately, they were ignoring me.

Part of that felt like I was being paranoid, but it seemed like the management office had turned colder since their angry letter.

Drip. Drip.

Another jagged hour of light sleep, more dozing than anything, remaining vaguely aware of larger beats of my environment, but missing the greater whole. The smoothness of the sheet, the warmth of the blankets, that feeling of holding your eyes closed in blackness when you wish to do anything but.

Consciousness remained just a moment away, if not already there.

Forty-five minutes more. My tablet, snugged into its clock dock, showed that it was both fully charged, and 4:17 AM, with an alarm set for 7:00 AM. There were two new series to watch on my StreamFX subscription, and it was going to be warm and sunny for November in San Jose today.

If I was coherent enough to read all that, I knew I was doomed. I was done with sleeping.

Rising, slipping my robe off my desk chair, I shrugged it on and wandered into the bathroom to catch a shower.

Thirty minutes under the warm stream of liquid relief provided a better resting environment than my bed had.

I brushed my teeth and went through my routine, dressing in fluffy grey sweats, a t-shirt with a cartoon otter hugging a fish and a heavy black hoodie.

Headphones left pocket, tablet in hoodie pocket; thick socks and sneakers, pretty much what every girl was wearing in the Netherlands this fall.

Pulling my hair back into a messy ponytail, content I was now the picture of fashion, I drifted into the kitchen and began making coffee, thudding down heavily in my chair while I waited for it to percolate.

That first, life-giving cup; the mysterious brown liquid of salvatory grace. 'Coffee... bring alertness to my weary synapses, it's going to be a long day.'

The best kind of long day. I smiled in raging defiance against the fatigue, as my anxiety and excitement surged then, in a feat of logic, took another sip of the popular stimulant. Who needs sleep when you can live on adrenalin?

The door opened, then shut quietly, the sound of a man breathing heavily.

John walked in fresh from a run, and badly in need of a shower.

"I hate you," I reported, taking a sip of coffee and pointing towards the pot.

He quickly gulped down a glass of water then made a straight line for the hot brown liquid.

"Good morning to you too, fish-breath," John replied, sitting down across from me.

"You know I don't like fish," I answered, distantly, still foggy from my wake up. "Have a nice run?"

"Yeah actually, always clears my head, but that fish thing, how does that work?" he challenged. It was a favorite tease.

"Yeah yeah, last time I checked, you weren't a vegan," I shot back in familiar defense.

"Ok, fair, but here's the thing. Will you like fish *tomorrow?*" His eyes flashed with an almost wicked intent, and his eyebrows rose, as he took a long pull from his own cup, a smirk riding into a smile across his face.

I almost dropped my cup, the idea hit me like a shock.

"I hadn't considered that, hmm, I guess we'll see." The smile ran away with me, and I found myself wiggling in my chair.

"Somebody's excited," he said, cooling down after his run.

"Well, duh," I replied.

"How are you holding up?" I asked, knowing that this had to be murder on him at some level.

"Oh I'm fine. Got my run in, got a lot of meetings set up for the Hague today, so I can be your ride in," he commented, talking about everything but what I was really asking about.

I know your tactics Mr. Dawkins, you cannot hide from me. Still, I got the point.

"Hey, buddy, do us all a favor, catch a shower," I teased.

"But I've already run so far and showers are so very quick," he replied in mocking tone, rising.

John appeared half an hour later in his dress grays, minus his blouse coat. The white dress shirt underneath was freshly cleaned and pressed.

"More monkey suit days," he said in passing. There was no taste in him for bureaucracy; in fact, the only time I had seen him close to happy, if bored, was when the Danube was on a deep space tour and the conversations came in on hour long delays.

"Thanks again for making the arrangements," I said, knowing he had to shuffle his schedule in advance.

"I'm mainly either at the Hague, Earth Central Command or sometimes Lunar One. It was just a matter of steering the meetings in the right direction," he replied, making excuses for his kindness.

"Still, thanks," I insisted, and he nodded.

"That all being said, I've got some things to go over before we get underway, so I better get to it,"

Just like that, I was again left alone with the noisy faucet...

Drip... Drip... Drip.

Dawn was fast approaching when an idea flashed, as I eagerly made my way outside to my tiny "patio".

The sun broke from the horizon, illuminating the sky in beautiful yellows, oranges and pink fluffy clouds. It was a fierce and beautiful sunrise, my last one trapped as a human being. The dawn of my first day.

Tears. I could not help the tears. Mixed with my fatigue, they made my eyes feel strange, but I openly wept.

There was only a hint of the coolness of the shifting season to come in the air, as the darkness gave way. There was a fresh dew upon the grass, and a few straggling birds still singing.

In the moment, it seemed like a perfect metaphor for my world.

My life had been a forest fire of all manner of emotions, experiences and agonies to this point, and today, the fire would end. Even now, it only smoldered, deprived of its ability to do any more serious damage.

Today, I won, finally. That one chance to become, to be, to correct the mistake I was saddled with at birth.

The last hour ticked by tortuously as I reveled in all the beauty of the dawn, enjoying every agonized moment.

Finally, impossibly, it was time. A quick trip on BART to Oakland International Spaceport near the sports stadium had us quickly in place at the Earth Central Command shuttle pad, where John's issued transport was kept.

"Come on, we're going to be late!" I charged up the ramp. There was no such thing as being early. I wanted to be there *now*.

"We're going to the Netherlands, not the moon. It's just an hour and a half from the shuttle pad. We're practically there already," he commented, sipping his coffee with sadistic intent.

"John. Please," I begged, all hope of dignity gone.

"Ok, geeze, I'm coming, I'm coming." He dragged himself dramatically up the shuttle ramp.

"I'll get my revenge on you one day Mr. Dawkins, when it's your turn to go through all of this." I thudded down heavily in the co-pilot's seat, crossing my arms in dramatic fashion, and made a face, childishly.

It had the desired effect; he choked on his coffee suppressing a laugh.

"Tell me again how you passed the psychological screening?" he asked absently, flipping switches on the small UEA transport shuttle he had been issued. It rumbled to life, metal creaking as it warmed unevenly. A slight, high-pitched whine briefly filled the corridor as something spun up.

"UEA-Orbital this is Bluebird-775 requesting orbital arc path into the Hague, United Earth Medical Center," John reported over the com briefly attending to business. He released a switch with his left hand and waited.

"Roger that Bluebird-775. Flight path is approved, and guidance has been downloaded. Safe flight."

The craft roughly leapt up, and then, as if discovering itself and its ability to fly, righted quickly, ascending up into the atmosphere.

"Sorry, a little rusty; used to the Danube." he commented.

The sky was rapidly darkening, and soon the curtain of the atmosphere pulled away, revealing the eternal night of space just behind the veil. The small craft seemed to level off as John flipped a few switches. Two lights illuminated on the dash. *Remote Guidance* and *Autopilot.*

The shuttle tilted of its own accord and aimed for a column of traffic following its flight-path.

"How long are your meetings today?" I asked. He was not only here for moral support, but had a job to do as well, which explained the dress grays he was wearing.

"Oh, just a few briefings today and then they are going to let me go. It's all I've been doing lately. Appointments here and there, more time in the shuttle than anything. It's weird after two years out there roaming." The craft drifted effortlessly as we entered with the rest of the orbital traffic; from my current vantage, I could see the rows ahead arcing up. We were nearing the halfway point.

"Is it really that different from being out there? You always complained that the days kind of bled together," I remarked, making idle conversation.

The craft slowly began its descent.

"Yeah, actually. The days do melt into one another out there; it's vast and beautiful but shockingly empty. It's kind of something you have to experience, but life has a rhythm to it, and after a while, it's just what you do, one thing to another. Suddenly, I'm back home and there're choices everywhere, options everywhere, something more than just duty, and rack time. It's kind of intense." It had become obvious in the last few months how much his time upon the Danube had shaped him.

An orbital transport drifted by. I watched it in silence, distracted for a time until it began to descend as it passed firmly out of my view.

"Was a lot of paperwork you were signing last night," John mentioned, warming up towards something.

"Formalities. It's not like I could say no." It felt like an offer I couldn't refuse. Sign or don't Shift. It was an easy decision.

"Still, maybe you should have a lawyer go over them or something." It had been a four hour marathon of sitting at the kitchen table, digitally signing forms with my data tablet.

Some of the text may have blurred together.

"It's already too late anyway and it's not like a lawyer would have told me it was a good idea to sign. They were all liabilities releases and wrongful death waivers and not one of that set would ever be willing give up the chance to sue anyone." I had other goals, and a new life waiting on a colony, which had made the papers seem trivial.

"I don't want to start this, not now. This is my last few hours of feeling good before I have a month long flu, this is no time to have an argument." Shift Tech was miraculous, but it came with a price; the first month on what they were calling "boosters" came with a ton of physical symptoms, from what they had seen in simulated trials.

"Fair point. I'm sorry," he admitted.

The craft glided gently down to the shuttle pad and he lowered the ramp.

"And by the way, congratulations," he offered, drawing a small otter plush toy out of a compartment just off the pilot's console.

"Someone to keep you company while you are sitting in that chair today getting IVs," he explained, handing it over.

"Aww John, it's perfect." I said, taking and tucking it into the crux of my left arm.

"Let me walk you in and then I have to get to my meeting," he replied, checking a watch he wore on his left wrist.

The weather was considerably cooler than back in San Jose. Zipping up my hoodie, I walked quickly along with John in tow. There was a curious noise growing as we got closer to the main medical center, turning the final corner. A large group of people surrounded the main entrance, holding protest signs.

"Save our Planet!" one read.

"Earth First!" said another.

The Crowd was chanting "humans only" over and over, as we walked through the protest line.

UEA Security had established a secure zone, but first, we had to get there.

It took another ten minutes of pushing through angry, shouting people, but finally, we got through to the checkpoint.

"State your business," said a guard, a sergeant.

"Appointment. Dr. Andropov," I replied. He briefly looked to John behind me, and saluted. John returned it.

He checked a digital clipboard.

"Ok, yeah, head on in," he said, clearing us.

John made certain I got safely in the building.

"I better go, going to barely make it with that crowd to fight back through. I'll contact you when I'm on my way back. Good luck," he said, turning to leave.

"Thanks" was all I had time for; he was already half way out the door. I realized in that moment that it was a tactical decision. Excuse or not, today was hard on him. I was moving forward while he was standing still. In a way, I felt pity. He was like a starving man that wouldn't eat.

He vanished out the door and then I was all on my own. My hands trembled as I took out my small tablet and connected to the hospital's network.

"Welcome to United Earth Medical Center" Flashed across the screen and presented me with a number of options.

Selecting "Patient Check-In", I stepped over to one of the local consoles and placed my hand on the pad while it interfaced with my tablet.

My details populated into the console screen. "Check in complete" flashed across my device and a map appeared. A blue indicator showed my location and a green one showed my destination.

Taking off down the hallway, I soon found myself in front of my second checkpoint of the day. This guy was a captain though, not a sergeant.

I suppose my time as an intern at JFA hadn't been completely useless after all.

He checked me in with a disdainful look and roughly indicated with his thumb behind him, telling me to move along. Scurrying past, I finally found myself in a normal waiting room, with a friendly, smiling receptionist that had to be five years north of sixty, ready to check me in.

"Oh hello dear. You're right on time. The protesters didn't give you too much trouble did they?" she asked, rising to get a number of old style paper forms, and attached them to a clipboard before handing them to me.

"Everything's fine. More forms? I checked in when I got here." A brief sense of fear gripped me, that there was some anomaly and I'd have to reschedule.

My heart sank.

Excitement had me on the razor edge of panic. Every statement had exaggerated intent, the lights seemed sharp and every sense was acute.

"Just a few last things for Dr. Andropov," she replied with a smile, and the despair quickly evaporated, my day redeemed.

"Thank goodness," I sighed, sitting down, tearing into the forms.

The minutes ticked by as I gave my medical history for the umpteenth time, and again filed out my vital statistics as best I knew. Finally I handed the completed forms back over to the granny receptionist and returning to my chair to nervously wait.

I subsequently played with my tablet, downloaded some magazines from the Hospital server and slowly felt as if I was going insane from waiting.

An hour ticked by. My appointment time well and truly exceeded, I slunk down into my chair, feeling depressed and sullen, as my chest tingled from anxiety all the while.

"Coswell, Joyce Coswell?" A nurse appeared in the door and I shot up as if rocket assisted.

"Here! Present!" I called out, a little too eagerly. My face flushed red in a blush and the nurse chuckled.

"Right this way miss," he said, gesturing to me.

We went through the normal doctor's office routine. Weight, blood pressure, vitals and my labs from the weekend were downloaded. Hum drum. The bureaucratic slowness of the medical system ate at my resolve; I was desperate for the moment, for it to start. It was supposed to be special dammit.

This felt like a trip to the Official Documents Bureau. The time dragged on interminably.

Ugh!

Finally, after another hour waiting in an examination room that seemed to be designed by artisanal closet makers, Dr. Andropov appeared.

Fresh air blew into the stale confines of my bored and bureaucratic day. Progress.

"Ah, Miss Coswell. Very sorry to keep you waiting so long. The protests have everything behind," he excused, in Russian-accented English. He was a tall man in his late 40s or early 50s, with salt and pepper hair. He wore a lab coat, dress pants and a dress shirt.. His thick black spectacles were a marked rarity; most people just got the shot.

"It's ok. I'm really excited," I admitted. My right hand's trembling probably giving it away. My left was occupied by the surprise gift John had given me.

"Let's see, now you understand that this process will be permanent for at least three years, correct? There is no stopping once you have begun." He asked, getting right down to business.

"Yes." He tapped a tablet he was holding in his left hand.

"And you understand that this is to shift your physical form to a sea otter... oh that explains your friend." He briefly addressed the stuffed animal.

"You are choosing what we are calling "feral". This is not fully approved and the full range of side effects are not known. This includes significant changes to your neural and physical architecture. You are doing this of your own free will, and you have been fully made aware of the risks," he continued.

"Yes." He tapped another two boxes.

"Ok. Last chance. Do you want to stop?" he asked, his eyebrows raised as if for emphasis.

"No. Not now, not ever. Let's do this," I replied, firm in my conviction. This was something I had been waiting my entire life for.

"It's fine. We just have to be sure," he said, pulling a small digital bracelet out of his right coat pocket and snapping it around my wrist.

"This will monitor the nanites in your system and relay the telemetry back here after we discharge you tomorrow; it will also serve as your ID and tracking for the program up until tanking. It cannot be removed, do you understand?" I nodded, after which he pulled out a small key and slid it into the bracelet; as it locked, three lights blinked across its front. It was black, and fit like a bangle. There was a tiny digital read out on the screen that resolved from the three dots to show my name, J. Coswell, and underneath it had the silhouette of an otter on it.

He led me to an elevator and we got onboard; pulling out a key card, he slid it into a slot. It soon after began to descend.

It opened on a deep sub-basement; stepping off, we walked down a hallway to a room full of green chairs that looked like knock-off versions of subpar recliners, all in their own kind of stall, he gestured to one. There were a few other people scattered about the large ward, but we were all far enough apart to make talking noisier than would be expected in a hospital setting.

IV bags hung from metal trees, and most people were listening to headphones or trying to sleep, ignoring the white walled, drab world surrounding them, as the contents of their bags slowly drained down.

It reminded me of my time working the oncology floor back in Nursing School.

I was next up on the list.

A nurse appeared and started two IV Lines one in each arm, then vanished, hardly saying a word, stopping only to scan my bracelet and check it against her tablet.

Fifteen minutes ticked by. Another nurse had two IV bags. She scanned them, then scanned my bracelet. Something on the screen turned green, and then reported audibly, "Bag contents verified. Deploy."

"Miss, take a few deep breaths for me," the nurse ordered, watching a screen just above my chair.

"Problem?" I asked.

"No, no problem, just relax. Your blood pressure just jumped ten points," she answered.

"Sorry, nervous," I replied; she chuckled, hanging the bags and setting the IV.

The first hour ticked by and I felt nothing except vaguely warm. Pulling my headphones out of my pocket, I plugged them into my tablet and began listening to music.

Another hour ticked by, the bags emptied and a different nurse soon returned and hung two more.

Then, the first wave of nausea hit. I looked left and looked right, found a large waiting bucket and lost what little breakfast I had.

I curled up in the chair, clung to my stuffed otter and tried to ride it out. I felt like pounded garbage. My head throbbed and my ears rang. The light stung my eyes and, though nauseous, I was also incredibly thirsty.

I asked for water, drank and found it to be a mistake, throwing up again, violently. Miserably, I turned off my music, curled into a ball, clung tighter to my stuffed otter and just waited.

I had never felt happier.

Chapter 6

The month of "fun" continued back home in San Jose.

Curled up on the couch with a 101 degree temperature, I watched cartoons in a semi delirious haze and flexed my stiff fingers. They were looking considerably more webbed these days, and I seemed to be growing a beard better than John as of late. Everything ached, and the changes were showing up in patches.

A chime beeped on my wrist device. My task master. Blearily, I rose, stumbling towards the kitchen and opened the fridge. I poured a white chalky liquid into a small measuring device and held my bracelet near it.

"Booster dose activated" flashed across its display. I chucked it down like it was fine tequila. Though cold at first, it always felt strangely warm going down.

Three weeks in, the worst was almost over, and I was getting accustomed to being sick. Machines, slowly picking apart and rearranging what they could, were doing this to me.

In one sense, my body was dying; in another, it was being rebuilt. It was amazing, and scary to watch.

I had already lost twenty pounds. My wardrobe was now relegated to things with drawstrings, and baggy t-shirts.

John eventually drifted by and poured himself a cup of coffee, he seemed to live off of it.

An urge built within me and a series of low contented grunts escaped my throat.

"Happy to see me?" he asked, eyebrow raised.

I blushed heavily. "I can't help it... yet? It's strange and kinda cool," I reported, briefly forgetting my soreness, and shifter flu.

He nodded. "I'm envious, I admit."

"You'll get your shot, someday, then I'll get to tease you," I replied.

"Hares aren't half as vocal as sea otters," he commented.

A wave of nausea hit and I ran quickly for the bathroom, losing the contents of my breakfast, but no trace of my booster dose. It was as if I had taken nothing at all.

Then, all I wanted to do was sleep.

Twelve blissful hours ticked by of deep inky blackness, followed by wild dreams full of strange esoteric notions and feelings almost like instinct. Swimming, so many dreams about swimming.

An incessant beeping was drilling its way into my head as I drifted happily on my back, the waves lapping over me in the dream.

My eyes snapped open; there was an intense and incessant vibration coming from my left wrist, providing physical accent to the noise.

"Booster" flashed across the screen.

"Yes master," I groaned, making my way towards the refrigerator.

It went down smoother than it had any right to. The stuff functioned on principles resembling witchcraft. It looked like antacid, tasted like nothing.

Alien snake juice.

Correction, otter juice...

I hoped.

It seemed to be going my way at least. An itching sensation suddenly blossomed to full awareness, intense and almost painful, coming from my left pinky, just under the fingernail.

Scratching at it, pulling gently, the nail let go with no pain, sliding free without effort.

I screamed.

"Joyce? What the fuck?" John cried, running in.

"Sorry, false alarm, more fun," I replied, breathing heavily. Small horrors like this were becoming part of my every day.

The things you have to get used to when you change your species...

"So you're ok?" he checked.

"Yes, just spooked," I assured, heart still fluttering. "I think I'll catch a shower."

"Can you run in your condition? They're very quick." He smiled at me as I glared, a low-throated growl erupted from me and he held up his hands.

"I'll get my revenge on you one day," I replied, turning and dragging my sore body to the bathroom.

The water fell like liquid relief, easing tension out of sore muscles. I sagged against the wall, like a puppet that had found new length to its strings. I did not notice at first when I lost four more fingernails.

I was simply too comfortable to care; I slid down, letting the hot water cascade over me.

There was a rude banging on the door that caused me to wake with a startle. The water had gone cold. Shivering, I shut it off, wrapping myself in a towel.

"Joyce, you've been in there an hour. Are you ok?" John asked, banging ever more frantically.

"I'm fine. You know the drill by now. I'm sorry," I mentioned apologetically.

"Just remember my sterling patience when it's my turn," he called out through the door.

Hunger... gnawing desperate hunger erupted, mainly for peanut butter. Don't ask me why.

Having a purpose to focus beyond the soreness and sick, I found myself heading directly for the kitchen and finding a jar.

I also found saltines. Two sleeves and half a jar of peanut butter later, I sat on the couch, watching cartoons, with the plate on my chest, nibbling my salty morsels as I held them in both my sightly webbed hands.

It was an ecstatic experience. My eating had been irregular, and in this brief and passing second, satiating my hunger was a rapturous emotion.

I ate them all. An immense amount of food, then found myself growing sleepy again, after which I promptly lost another block of time to Morpheus.

Chapter 7

I had survived the month of fun, or maybe I had simply gotten accustomed to being sick.

Five weeks in, and it was early December; the holiday party was next week, and the festive decorations filled the store while the torturous music assaulted my ears.

Moving through the supermarket, I felt like a wraith. My bony frame clearly visible having lost another twenty pounds. There was no white left to my eyes, having darkened to black, with hints of soulful brown. A heavy goatee of whiskers erupted out from my face, and my webbed hands looked somewhat disfigured, in mid-change. Holding things was becoming difficult, but I could still push a shopping cart.

"Freak," a fellow patron said, smacking his shoulder into me in challenge as he went by.

I suppose these things happen.

"Fuck....you... buddy..." I whispered quietly under my breath. I didn't want to start a fight, not really, but also, talking was becoming serious work. Something about my throat didn't want to move right anymore.

It was something that was expected to happen at some point in the process, but this was happening sooner than planned; everything was happening on a somewhat accelerated schedule to what I had been told, but I didn't care, it was just something to mention at my visit to the doctors office in a few hours.

John walked up and dropped a few things in the basket. We had learned to do our shopping before the clinic trips; afterwards, I was normally too tired.

"Wrap it up fish breath, we got a schedule to keep," John urged.

I paused, taking the time to form the words. "Screw... you... Hoppy."

He laughed. I was going to have so much fun tormenting him when it was his turn. I couldn't wait.

We were in the checkout line when a manager walked up to us; he addressed John first, who was in uniform.

"Excuse me, uh sir, but could we ask your friend to wait outside, she's... it's a she right? She's scaring our guests," he mentioned in a halting and apologetic tone. My face blushed under my hood and I could not help but feel ashamed.

"Ask her directly, have the fucking balls or step off. You want to be a prick? You don't get to be a coward," John spat, his anger clearly visible.

I could *smell* it, just as surely as I could smell the manager's fear.

"John, it's fine. I'll wait outside," I said, excusing myself.

"No," he replied firmly. I didn't want to create a scene, but he was ready to start a war.

"Sir, I need to ask you to calm down," the manager insisted, security was on their way over.

"Ask... her... directly," John replied, slowly.

"Miss, I'm going to have to ask you to leave," he announced, finally relenting.

My voice was too sore and raspy to work out a quick response.

"Fuck this place, you don't need our cred," John spat, and we both stormed out.

"The fucking nerve of that place." His form was rigid, as he stomped out into the parking lot, beside himself with anger. He pulled out his data tablet and jabbed with his finger, selecting through his apps, summoning a car from the transport service.

"It's... fine...he was afraid... Could tell." I grasped at my throat. It was seriously hurting to force the words.

64

The Oakland International Spaceport was becoming a familiar sight. Weekly trips at odd times had me recognizing the guards on duty at the checkpoints.

The drama of the morning, combined with Shift Tech had me feeling exhausted; I collapsed into my seat in the shuttle and slept all the way to United Earth Medical.

Before I knew it, I was back in the exam room developed by artisanal closet makers.

"And how are we doing today?" Dr. Andropov asked as he entered.

"Lots... Changes... Hard... Talk," I reported, and his eyebrows raised as he made some notes in his clipboard.

"Interesting, we are a few weeks ahead of where we're projected to be," he offered in a neutral clinical tone, pulling out a pen light, checking my eyes and then feeling for a pulse.

"Problem?" I worked out, before wincing.

"I don't think so; going over the telemetry data from your wrist monitor, everything is good and you are medically stable. It's always a little different from the scenarios, everybody is different, even simulated ones," he explained.

I nodded.

"I'll be right back, just a moment." He disappeared for about fifteen minutes and then returned, holding a strap in his hands with a box attached to the front.

"You should have been briefed on these in the orientation. Voice Collars. As your anatomy loses the ability to control resonance in your throat and those features change, voice box or not, it's going to become increasingly difficult to speak. Sea otters are very vocal, as I'm certain you know, but they have nothing on human vocal communication."

He handed it to me; it was a black generic model, and would work well enough for my purposes. I flexed it back and forth in my webbed hands and pulled it across my neck. It snapped home with a magnetic click finding its slot.

That was clever. I should be able to manage that even with my hands becoming more mitten-like, which they were with every passing day.

"Jumping right in I see, well I suppose that's understandable," he chuckled.

"Nervous, scared, tired, angry...." A series of noises and words erupted out of the collar, then a high pitched whine that threatened to split my head.

"Easy dear, you have to learn to control it; hold the words in your mind, and then focus on speaking. It's going to be a conscious deliberate decision, and imperfectly executed until your brain learns to map to the new hardware. We're throwing a lot of changes at it. Patience." He made excuses, but I did not mind; even these challenges carried a thrill.

I was on the frontier, it was costing me convenience and luxuries I had always enjoyed, but what I was gaining was so much more. Voice collars didn't matter, stiff forepaws didn't matter, neither did the limitations in access.

Being myself mattered. It only became clearer as the month wore on, and I looked more and more like a disfigured monster. The sense of detachment to my body only grew, all while I began to identify intensely with parts of it.

I loved the patterns in the webbing of my fingers, the random twitching of my whiskers and how they caught the slightest breeze.

The price was high, but it came with admission to a world of wonders and freedom.

"Sandwhiches," I said through my collar and sighed, dramatically conveying my failure.

"Thank... you..." I rasped out. The doctor chuckled.

"Keep at it, you will get it," he encouraged.

Smiling revealed the new gaps from a few missing teeth.

"The process is greatly accelerating, more than with the rest of the group, probably due to the degree of changes involved. There's a lot more to do. That being said, I'd like to rearrange your tanking schedule. Let's move you in on the first of February, instead of month-end." He made a few notes in his clipboard, as every sense I had suddenly focused in on him.

The idea excited me. The last hard day; after that, it was just a matter of floating peacefully in a deep coma for six months.

"Good," the collar reported, to which he smiled.

"See, you've begun to get it already," he remarked and a happy chitter escaped my throat, making those noises no longer hurt.

"Remarkable." He checked a few more boxes off his digital form and guided me back towards the elevator to the subterranean ward.

"Now remember, it is very important that you keep up with your booster doses," he chided, which reminded me of my curiosity.

"What-do?" It seemed strange, that part of the process was never fully explained. What had to be taken every twelve hours that couldn't be achieved by these IV sessions?

"They are the diagnostic bots that communicate with your bracelet. Because of the alien biotech in your system, they only last about twelve hours. It's vital you keep up with them to keep us apprised of your condition." He lined it out and I nodded in agreement.

"Doing, purple... Raptors..." My voice collar reported. *The hell?*

The doctor laughed, losing his sense of professional detachment briefly. Then he lead me into the familiar ward with it's familiar recliner, always the same stall, one nurse, then another.

Dance of the Shift Tech.

"Keep practicing," Dr Andropov said, before quickly scurrying away; my ears caught the sound of additional chuckling as he made his way down the hall.

Pulling out my tablet, I began listening to my music and set a timer for forty-five minutes.

I had this part down. When the nurse hung the first bag, I tapped the start button with my right fore paw.

Melting into the music, I waited. The time ticked down.

Forty-five minutes sounded, then I quickly put the tablet away and removed my headphones.

Any moment now...

The sudden contracting wave of cold, then the gut punch.

And bucket on the right as always.

It's amazing the things you can get used to.

Chapter 8

I sat up on the couch at home, looking around, having little memory of the trip home from the clinic. It came in foggy recollections; there was a voice in the room with me... talking to me.

"Hungry... Food... Hungry..." was on repeat from my collar.

"Booster..." added to the chorus; my left fore paw was buzzing. I chirped angrily at the noise.

"Shut the fuck up..." I said through the collar without intention, quickly tapping the bracelet twice, acknowledging my task.

Something felt strange... stranger than normal. I was *hot*.

Moving to the bathroom, I stripped down. There was a fine black soft coating of underfur covering my skeletal frame. The heavy cotton trapped too much heat. It was neither thick, nor complete, but it was *fur*. Real fur.

My fur. All worry of soreness gone, replaced by a surging, soaring happiness.

"Booster. Booster" rang out again from my wrist device, breaking me out of my celebrations.

"Ok, let's get organized. Booster, then shower, then shirt. On second thought, a bath would be nicer," I said out loud through my collar, not intending to.

"Stop saying what I'm thinking," I again said to myself. It did not listen.

"Twelve hours and I could barely get it to work, now I can't get it to shut up," I continued.

"Ahhh this is so frustrating, it's repeating everything I think. Cantaloupes… bookends... Kumquat!" John then banged on a wall.

"Keep it down will ya? Trying to work in here," I ducked my head sheepishly and chittered.

I unfastened it, and set it down, tired of broadcasting every thought. There would be plenty of time to play after the morning's chaos was managed.

Aside from the impossibly thin coating of underfur down my front torso and back, with strips in irregular patches down my arm, my jaw was sore, and it was hard to close my mouth all the way.

It made the booster dose particularly challenging; some of it dribbled down my chin, but when I went to clean it up, it had already gone, apparently absorbed transdermally. Once active, they seemed to know where they wanted to be.

Human spy juice.

I eyed breakfast suspiciously, and instead opted for a bath. Everything was sore today, and there was an increasing feeling of being fully out of calibration. Nothing moved exactly right, felt exactly right or worked exactly right.

Slipping into the hot bath, I drifted for about an hour before emerging to work on colony business.

I had to set the paper portion aside, until I had help. The webbing between my fingers was forcing them closer together, and my thumbs were already heavily immobilized. My hands resembled paws more by the day, with the loss of function to match, even showing the beginning of the pads-congruent with otters of my species.

Doors were becoming a real issue, and I was becoming more dependent on John, as well as assistive devices as the time went on.

Experiencing the cost of it, put it in a much deeper light. There were so many things I had taken for granted, even being able to comb out my hair. Well, whatever hair I had left. It was falling out in clumps and being replaced by the same fine coating of underfur, only lighter. Still, it went further.

I couldn't handle pens well at all, and had about the same luck with silverware. Even the way I ate had to change, and was changing. New habits were taking over, coming out of left field; subtle nudges that were hard to realize were new at all. As odd as it appeared, and often felt, it also felt strangely... normal.

There was no recognizing myself in the mirror anymore. With each passing day, I looked more like the animal I had always seen myself as, and wanted to be.

It was like watching myself become more myself. Every day of my shift I became more of a complete person, less saddled by the curse that was my birthright.

There was another change, deeper, my mentality. There was a building need to play. More things seemed like games. There was an eagerness for new challenges.

Anything that was a game was certainly worth playing.

Voice collar. That's right, I was going to play with that. Forgetting completely about work, I sought out my own fun.

Fumbling, it took about ten minutes, but I managed to get it on by myself, which felt like a victory.

"Testing, 1... 2..." It seemed to be working.

"Enhyrda Lutris. Conservation status, recovering." I tried to think but not say, but failed.

"Damn." Another failure.

"Son of a bitch."

...

"Try to think without making words go."

"It's supposed to be hard to turn on, why is it hard to turn off?" I asked the ghosts rhetorically, my thoughts on full display.

There was a sharp stabbing pain behind my eyes, and everything went out of focus for a moment.

The collar made a strange noise right afterward.

Hello? I tried it, nothing.

Testing, can anyone hear me? Nothing.

Dammit feast or famine. I thudded my head down frustrated and heard a noise in the kitchen, to which I moved to investigate.

John had a tool box with him. Duct tape was set out on the table, one roll on top of another, as well as a ball of twine and a box cutter.

"You know, I really should have recorded the shuttle ride home last night. You're fun delirious. Man, the dreams you were having," he chuckled, enjoying his private mystery, driving me to full and rabid curiosity.

That strange pain, the itch behind my eyes again, a strange wail through the collar then the flood.

"Hi John, what's that, you asshole, what did you hear, food?" It came all at once, rushing out as a torrent.

To his credit, he tried. He fell to a fit of uproarious laughter, dropping one of the spools of tape across the floor.

74

There was this curious urge to chase it, for the sheer joy of it that seized me, which quickly passed.

"Ok, find your zen, try to focus on the words only," I told myself, outside of my head, ignoring my own monologue.

"Harder... Than ... it ... looks to control." The effort to speak normally sapped what shallow energy reserves I had and I plopped down to the floor.

"You ok?" he asked, quickly rising.

"Fine... stop, stop." I held up my right paw.

"Rest."

He nodded.

"Art... project?" I forced out, gesturing towards the table.

"Observe," he said, rising.

"I did some reading off the net today. Got some ideas," he continued, crossing over to the pantry door.

Opening it, he taped the latching mechanism down, so that it could not engage. Then he tied a loop into the length of a rope, tying the other end around the door.

"I'm off till the middle of December. Danube is going in for a retrofit, so I'm finally getting some shore leave. Thought I'd retrofit the apartment a little bit, because I'm not going to be here much next month."

"Good idea... will manage... having fun," I smiled, feeling my whiskers move.

He chuckled. "The dexterity thing has me worried."

"Not so bad. Still have a thumb. Kinda." I worked the webbed digit, now heavily restricted by its connections, as if in demonstration. It was a far cry from what I once had, but it served for most functions. I could grasp things with a bit of effort, and had more flexibility than a normal otter had.

Another new way of working with the world.

"Fair enough." He looked around the kitchen, as if in thought.

"What's your final projected height, or is it length?" he asked, with his hands on his hips.

"Four foot, five inches. About a foot down from where I am now. Well was, I've lost a little bit of height, but not much." Holy shit, I felt pride as it came from the collar perfectly. With all of the changes it was kind of like being a teenager again. Soreness in the morning and minor subtle changes to the environment, slowly altering everything.

"When are you going metric with the rest of the world?" John teased.

I did the math in my head.

"1.37 meters." and then there was that grin of his again.

"Yeah, was afraid of that," he said, getting data he could work with.

"We need to move things down from the higher spots, especially if I'm not going to be here next month."

It was a playful, working, afternoon. After placing a delivery order for a number of three tiered shelves that would soon line the apartment like some strange fencing along the walls, John busied himself duct-taping down latches to doors and tying threads around door knobs.

The time passed, the shelves came as expected. The paper skyscrapers that formed out of stacks on the living room table now had a competition in box-pile-ville.

He worked, I supervised.

"I'm hungry," he announced, finishing the last shelf and setting it to one side. Tomorrow would be rearranging day.

"Me too," I chittered. It was my normal state now, somewhere between hungry and dying of starvation.

"Burger?" he offered.

"Fish," my voice collar reported. I hadn't meant to say that.

But in that moment, I fiercely wanted one.

"Excuse me?" and then the grin appeared.

A small distant part of me, like a half forgotten memory, wanted to gag thinking about it.

"Yes... Fish... Hot damn... Fish...Now... uh please?" I stammered through my collar, in spite of myself.

Chapter 9

Like a revelation brought from the heavens themselves...

I had discovered tuna.

It came at a fortuitous time, the sickness was largely passed, except for sudden violent waves of illness. Most of the time, I was just incredibly sore and incredibly hungry.

Skittering over to the shelf, I took hold of the dangling flat head screwdriver attached to it by a length of twine. Working it awkwardly in my paw, I managed to maneuver into a position where I could use my rudimentary thumb to hold it firmly in between the pads. It was vaguely uncomfortable, but I was getting accustomed to it.

Grip achieved.

Working it under the pull tab, it popped away; the scent causing me to tremble with hunger.

Repeating the same trick with a plastic knife, I was able to get it out of the can without too much mess.

Retrieving a few wet wipes from the pull box, I was soon set on the couch, with a plate on my chest, happily eating it with my hands.

The idea that this could have ever been disgusting seemed as foreign as a pink sky.

It was *ambrosia.*

Greedily, I devoured the entire plate. I may have licked it. *I admit nothing.*

Eyeing the shelf full of cans, and briefly considering another, I dismissed it, sat and began cleaning my paws with the wet wipes, before grooming and rubbing those same clean paws against my muzzle and face, all as a contented fit of chitters escaped my throat. My world calmed, as I fell to rhythmic, instinctual action.

Successful lunch, now for a nap and some cartoons.

In spite of all the soreness, and the vomiting the last few days, it had felt more like a vacation than anything. It was all coming together, and best of all, for the first time, I actually liked myself.

Don't get me wrong. I've always liked who I am, the otter inside of the human cage, but the body... the strange, hulking mass of chains that was always a barrier to that expression had faded to a ghost. The real me now shined through in my eyes, my whiskers and the cream-colored fur that covered my face and head.

I began to recognize myself in the mirror, for the first time, seeing not a stranger, not some hellish costume that was stuck upon me like some horror movie, but *me... The real me.*

Joy is not the word, nor is elation. Contentment comes close, or satisfaction, but there was an overwhelming *rightness* to being that had never existed before, giving me a foundation I never had.

The world, for all its hurts and challenges was more vibrant, more bright and more alive than I had ever imagined, all while, I lost my ability to speak, open doors or even write without help.

The astounding and revelatory enlightenment of being made, made any cost seem paltry and, thus, I reveled in all of it.

A half hour spent vomiting over the commode was a half hour where the sickness was being purged out of me. The soreness in my bones was my body coming alive as if animated by some new truth.

Slowly, desperately and rapturously, I was becoming a whole person.

John began to stir on the other side of the apartment. I hung my paws over the couch, and peaked up over the back of it, in hiding perch, watching for his entrance.

He emerged wearing his duty uniform. All kitted out.

I chittered in confusion.

"Aren't you on shore leave?" I asked, perking up over the couch. He walked by and fuzzled the fur on my head, causing me to emit a pleased chirring noise.

"That's adorable," he commented.

I blushed under my fur.

"You'd think they'd at least give me a weekend, I knew I wouldn't get three weeks," he said, monologuing as much as talking.

"Why? Will you be back for the Christmas party?" I asked, in rapid succession.

"I won't know why till I get there, just got orders to report. Pretty sure it's the Mendians. Every time we spot one of their ships, Central Command takes that as a reason to get the First Contact team together. All I did was verify star charts. I'm no diplomat," he complained.

"You signed up," I teased.

"I'll remember your compassion the next time you're vomiting at 0400," he responded with a humorous tone.

Ducking behind the couch, I hid, playfully.

"Ok, ok. Will you be alright here?" he asked, switching subjects.

"Go. It's not been a bad week for my symptoms and I've plenty of fish to keep me fed," I replied. Another can sounded lovely at the moment.

"Yeah, but your hobbling more, kind of limping," he said. My gait had been altering slightly as my hind flippers began to catch up with my fore paws.

"That's only going to get worse till I've gone full quadruped and that won't happen until after the tank," I reminded.

"Not reassuring," he replied, checking his watch nervously.

"Go. Everything is set up, I'll be fine," I urged.

Reluctantly, he reached over, fuzzled my head fur once more and left.

An eerie calm descended upon the apartment.

Tapping my tablet, aiming to strike it with my forward most paw pad, because it could easily register it, a chime erupted.

"StreamFX. Cartoons. My List," I repeated clearly through the collar.

I was getting good with it, most of the time.

Insane levels of animated violence soon ensued upon my screen as the canary predictably handed out the pain to the cat once again.

It was all old hat, but that wasn't the point.

Two more cans of tuna down as I drifted in a haze on the couch; the noise from the screen bled into the background. All was warm and content in my world.

A brief, sharp knock punctuated through the apartment, bringing a calamitous and panicked end to my warm day dreams.

With an animalistic yelp, moving faster than I had the right to, I dove over the couch, and took refuge behind the armrest, putting it between me and the door

An envelope slid in and the person walked off. I peeked over my hiding place with curiosity raging, as I focused in upon it.

Moving to investigate, taking it up in my paws, the mystery deepened when I saw it was from my apartment complex.

It wasn't sealed, so I shook out the letter inside and smoothed it out on the floor, reading it.

"Notice to Vacate, End of Month." Was all it said.

No reason cited, no cause given, just, time to leave.

Fuck

It couldn't have come at a worse time.

Was this even legal?

Descending upon my tablet, I did what I could to become an instant expert in tenant law.

I was screwed. On month to month rentals, they had to give a minimum of two weeks' notice; the closing date on the apartment, hit that minimum exactly.

And John was gone until at least next week. *What was I going to do?*

Panic. A moment of pure unadulterated panic. This had been my home for two years. I needed it, had paid for it and hardly asked for anything.

The faucet dripped as if in testimony of my words, representing two months of ignored maintenance requests.

The earlier complaint. My eyes narrowed.

The panic flashed to anger.

Tapping the speaker icon on the tablet once again, the chime toned.

"Call, apartment office!" I ordered.

"Dolphin Bay Apartments, Marcia speaking, how can I help you?" A friendly, if generic receptionist answered over the line.

I focused intently on my words and my control, not wanting my voice collar to get in the way.

"Hi, this is Joyce Coswell in 32c. I just got a notice to vacate, I've been up on my rent and have no complaints on me lately, just want to know what's going on." My demeanor was a facade, inwardly I was burning down villages.

"Just a moment," she said. The line clicked, once, then twice.

"Management, this is Clark." A gruff voice reported over the line.

Again, I went over the details.

"Oh, yeah. You need to be out by the end of the month," he confirmed, offering nothing.

"But why? I haven't done anything." I asked, my tone, insistent.

"I don't have to give you an explanation. I've already given you notice." The line went dead.

Disbelief. Two years, never late on rent, only one complaint, months ago.

The reason was clear. And it had started off as such a nice day.

A call into the Central Command switchboard to try and raise John proved equally fruitless. Citing security protocols, it was a long shot; I wasn't listed as family and it wasn't a pressing emergency. Another dead end.

I looked around, looked left and right, in a futile quest for direction. Seeing only how much there was to pack, how much there was to do.

Where was I going to go?

John had a cabin in British Columbia. He had inherited it when his father had died.

Still, that was no guarantee, and it wasn't exactly the place for me in my current state. Having direct access to services, for the moment, was incredibly important.

Then there was my work for the colony committee; while it was getting done, it was moving at a crawl. In spite of my inability to fill out all the forms, I needed to be here.

No job, tank in a little under two months, living on my savings and unemployment.

What the fuck was I going to do?

Storm clouds roared in, a hurricane disrupted my sunny vacation as emotions sent me into a tumult.

The rejection stung as much as the uncertainty. What did I ever do to them? What was so wrong about me that they had to hate me so much?

I'm only an otter. There's nothing scary about me.

Memories of the first month of my shift, the sagging skin, the missing fingernails, the black eyes on an otherwise, mostly human face. Kronenberg days.

Maybe I was a little scary.

The thought depressed me and I pushed it away. My change was beautiful and it always had been, even if they couldn't see it.

Fucking humans.

Why did everything have to be so complicated?

Chapter 10

Half the cans of tuna were gone, the recycling was overflowing and I was no closer to finding a new place to stay.

I had not left my apartment in three days.

For one, I was having extreme difficulty manipulating the doorknob to the exterior, but that wasn't the sole issue. There was a sliding patio door, I could have used it.

In truth, I was afraid. The eviction was hitting like a more passive form of assault. Someone was burning my world down legally, just as the thugs had burned down the community center physically.

It was impossible to divorce those two events from each other in my mind. They both seemed to stem from the same kind of bias that came with my changes, an animation towards cruelties both tangible and intangible.

Regardless of the action, the result was the same. Damage, pain and stress everywhere.

I did not even know how to begin packing in my current state. There were times when opening a tuna can required a nap.

For the last three days, I had brooded, as I lived in my changes and my cartoons, the outer world- a distant concern.

The noise of keys sliding into locks brought my insular bubble to a sudden end.

John emerged through the door.

"Hey fish breath," he said, the nickname now appropriate.

I forgot all my troubles as a surge of joy went through me, and I chirred contentedly.

"Friend!" my collar exclaimed excitedly, without intention. Emotions did the strangest things to it, sometimes focusing it, sometimes turning it into a shotgun blast of my thoughts.

"It's good to see you." I focused on the words, forgetting briefly my problems.

"What's this?" He asked, and picked up the notice from the apartment on the entrance side table.

Oh shit.

His sunny disposition vanished as he crumpled the piece of paper into one hand, his eyes blazing with fire.

"John, easy. Let's talk," I urged, everything about his body language terrifying me in that moment.

There was a smell to it too. I couldn't ignore it. Acrid.

"Was going to tell you about it tonight. Didn't want it to go like this," I admitted.

"What reason did they give?" He spat.

"They didn't. They aren't required to, legally. I got the notice a few hours after you left, nothing we can do," I admitted.

John remained in the entrance way, seething.

"Come in, sit down and get control," I ordered. This was familiar territory. John was good-natured to a fault, but there was a deep and hidden anger that he had fought, and hated about himself as long as I had known him. A lifetime in an ill-fitting cage does strange things to people.

We both knew its truest source; the indignities, the injustices of the world, brought it to frothing boil.

"Fine." He snapped and slammed the door behind him. The noise hurt my ears.

It was progress, at least.

He stormed out to the patio and remained silent, looking up at the sky for the next fifteen minutes, as if searching for something.

Returning, he had found his calm, and was all about business.

"Ok. So we need a plan, and we need somewhere to go. I've got the cabin in BC. It's not perfect but it's a fall back; have you reached out to your parents?" he asked.

"Not in months; the second I signed up for the trial, I got an email about how hard this was for them and they were going to need time. They have their condo on Mars, and the distance has always been good for us, you know that," I replied, not wanting to even think about that conversation.

"Hey, I haven't talked to my Mom since Dad died, I know how that is. She went waaay off the deep end," John recollected with a sad laugh.

"You never really talk about that." Our conversation had pivoted strangely, but it was clear he needed the support.

"Don't like to. Hadn't heard from her in over five years until I got home. She saw me on the news. First contact team."

"Was she happy, proud of you I bet?" It was a natural assumption, but the look on his face said otherwise.

"Ashamed. Said I helped sell out the species. Reminded me that Manhattan was bought for beads and cost the tribe everything. She lost all trust in everything after Dad passed." He paused briefly, then took a deep breath.

"Enough of that. I don't like to think about it. So, what are our options?" he asked, switching the subject.

"I'm going to ask tomorrow at the Christmas party, leverage that colonial spirit," I replied, as I flashed a grin.

"Good plan, snaggle tooth," he remarked.

"Snaggle tooth?" I cocked my head.

"You've got some pointy ones coming in there," he replied.

With a plan in place and the situation temporarily diffused, he soon left to unpack.

It seemed a futile gesture, considering.

Chapter 11

The apartment and its contents had detonated everywhere in a cacophony of chaos, but I had greater concerns at the moment. The day had come for the Christmas party.

"Where's my hoodie?" I called out through my collar to the air, chittering with the effort. There was a whole new assortment of clicks, barks and chirps that was accenting my speech as of late, as my throat moved towards more animalistic directions; my collar kept me anchored in the human world.

"Look under the boxes in the dining area," John replied, referencing the paltry scrap of space between the kitchen and living room.

Hobbling over, working my developing flippers, I found it under the last empty box.

"Found it, we have to get going, quit primping," I coaxed.

He stepped out in his dress grays, cleaned and pressed.

"You're overdressed, no need to be so formal," I chided, wiggling into my hoodie, I was hardly wearing anything underneath, but a thin spaghetti strap top and a light skirt, my fur doing the job sufficiently while I was indoors.

Even in San Jose, it was December. Often, this was the rainy and cold season, when the weather cooperated. This year, it did, and the temperatures were cooler than normal.

The weather let me get away with baggier clothes that hid the bulk of my strange appearance; only my face gave it away, looking considerably more otter-ish than human as of late.

My jaw was still lost as to how to fully function, but the tip of my nose had blackened and was pulling up slightly. My ears pulled in more to the sides of my head and were losing their lobes. My eyes had changed in the first month, and so, now with my fur in, and my hair gone, I looked a strange mix, but not garish or horrible; most of the time I could hide under my hood.

Swimming in my baggy clothes, I was down to ninety-five pounds, from a former one-sixty. I had to pause for a moment and catch my breath after all the sudden activity.

"You ok?" He checked in, ever vigilant.

"Yeah, just fine Hoppy, but we better get going," I urged.

The hall was attached to a motor inn, now an antique from the age of nations, when this was the United States, instead of North America, Sector 2.

A few cars occupied the parking lot, with a truck and shuttle parking across the street.

"Fifty credits huh? Is that for the hall, or by the hour," John commented, with that wicked grin of his.

"Be nice, he's been very to kind to us," I insisted.

"Just saying," he excused.

"It's just old, but it looks lovingly maintained. I think its living off the small space sport nearby," I remarked.

We entered what, in some ways, was a monster's ball. Morphics in various states of change milled about the hall. Kevin bounced like the kangaroo rat he was becoming, had rounded ears and shiny black eyes. Sonya was sporting a red panda mask, and was holding her paws at chest level out front. It was the first time we had seen each other since the beginning of our changes.

"Joyce! Wow!" Ricky said, moving over to greet me, stooping down in a hug. "You're wasting away girlie."

"Radical weight loss plan," I commented, then continued. "Life changing."

"Pointy teeth too, kind of like me." Ricky smiled wide showing new, fierce teeth, which stood out proudly against his now black lips, and ocelot patterned fur.

John had the strangest look on his face, almost as if he was hurting. He excused himself, and went outside.

I didn't want to push. Fearing that this party might be hard for him, I elected to give him space.

"He ok?" Ricky commented.

"Yeah, will probably be walking the same path soon." The words spoke volumes.

"Ah," Ricky got it.

"So how are things?" He continued, trusting me to handle John.

"Personally, never better. My life, however, is going a bit crazy. I'm getting evicted. Pretty certain it's because of all this," I indicated to myself.

"Yeah, have you been keeping up with the news? It's getting hot out there," Ricky mentioned.

"No. Been ignoring it as hard as I can. It's not too difficult, I sleep twelve hours a day minimum."

"Aye that's me too, and I'm not even shifting as far as you are either," he went on.

"You know, I'm retired, got a rusted out old shuttle and have a place up in Norcal. Why don't you pack up and stay with me? Sonya would love the company; I like to tinker alone in my shop, and the more she shifts, she just gets quieter. It would probably be good for her," Ricky mentioned.

"You sure?" My world brightened.

"It makes sense. We are the three people working on the colony. Gives us a chance to get a lot done before we tank. Maybe." We both laughed at that. There were days when you woke up ready to conquer the world, and days when you woke up feeling about two steps from death.

Every time I slept, it was a coin flip as to how waking up would feel.

"Well ok then. That does work out. Ricky, thanks, I don't know what to say." Tears streaked down my fur. I was still capable of crying like a human.

For some reason, the thought vaguely annoyed me.

"Aww buddy, come here." He knelt down and hugged me as I chirred contentedly. "Always had a penchant for picking up strays."

I couldn't help but smile, and excused myself to find John, to relay the good news.

Something popped in my left flipper on the way out the door, and then my knee went out from under me. I began to fall.

A bespectacled, older man, easily in his late sixties, rushed over and caught me.

"Easy miss." Though old, he was obviously strong, and prevented my descent; my weight sagged against him as I righted myself. My hood fell down.

"Whoa," he responded, and took a step back.

"Thanks. Uh, I'm sorry." I quickly replaced my hood.

"No that's alright. You're Joyce right? Your fur is beautiful. We spoke on the phone, I'm Steve Berkowitz, was coming to check in on the party." He held out his hand in introduction and I offered my left paw in return.

He gracefully took it and shook, rolling with my appearance in perfect stride.

Cautiously, I let my hood down.

"So why is your fur on your head a different color?" he asked, without preamble.

"It's how it is with my species, sir. Kind of cream-colored at top, and a deep brownish black from the neck down or so. It is just the way we're made." The questions made me feel special. He was curious, not afraid or disgusted.

"Fascinating. Questions are ok right?" he asked, after the fact.

"Of course. Seems the least I can do for the Hall," I gestured back.

"Oh, this old thing has been in my family for three generations now. My grandfather bought it in 1962, back in its glory days; before humans were on the moon ya know, I mean ever, not just living," he clarified.

"I learned that in school. Wasn't it Jim Lovell and Apollo 13? One small step for man?" I asked, trying to remember Junior High history.

"Close. I'm impressed. That was Neil Armstrong and Apollo 11. God, how the times have changed," he remarked.

I pulled my tablet out of my pocket to check for messages from John.

"And some things never do," he smiled, mysteriously.

"So don't let me keep you out here all night, everyone is waiting to greet you. I need to go find someone and then I'll be right in," I said. There was a strange feeling to my world, a rising oddness I couldn't place.

I found him across the street in shuttle parking, staring up at the sky as he was prone to doing.

Safe. Hungry... Fish... Friend... Need... Strange place

I was having a hard time focusing. My thoughts coming in more like waves. Everything was falling into natural rhythms.

"Hi. Friend. Ok? Hungry? Need food?" The word were disjointed and it was hard to pick the right ones.

A set of nervous barks escaped my throat.

"Uh Joyce? You ok?" John asked. Something seemed wrong with him.

Instinct pushed me closer. I nuzzled into his chest and pressed close with a happy chirr.

"Safe. Ok," I insisted.

"I'm not liking this." John observed, I was doing everything right, why wasn't he responding?

My world flashed and suddenly everything clicked back into place.

"Whoa. That was *intense*." It felt almost like a drug. The entire world melted away into an ever-present-now for the briefest of seconds.

"Mind letting me in on it? John asked.

"Uh... How to describe it. There was instinct and rhythm, and thought was there; but calm, on the back burner, watching more than doing." The full description was impossible to capture with words.

"Your speech got weird and spaced, I'm taking you in," he said, panic on the edge of his voice.

I caught whiff of it, and I snapped off again, nuzzling back up to John, chittering, trying to comfort him, as I sensed more distress in his scent, and posture.

He took out a rectangle from his pocket and began playing with it. That looked like a fun game.

"Hello, is this the Emergency Beta Hotline? We have a problem." He was making strange noises now. What was wrong? I barked in concern.

It could be dealt with later, I felt tired and comfortable curled up with him. A nap was in order.

Chapter 12

"Joyce? Joyce? Can you hear me?" asked a heavily Russian-accented voice. There was a bright light in my eyes.

"Yes." My thoughts were moving like frozen jello. "What... happened?"

"You had a neurological event dear. Welcome back," he congratulated. The light, mercifully left my eyes.

Sitting up and looking around, I recognized the smells of the United Earth Medical Center.

"How long have I been here?" John was sitting in a corner, a look of deep concern on his face.

"About a day, but everything is fine, and will be fine. Remember you are a pioneer," he reminded.

"So tell me what's happening!" I ordered, not wanting to be placated.

"As you know, you are among our first 250 and our first feral. The process, as a result, has been much more intensive for you than the rest and we suspected this. However, during the simulated trials, there was no surge," he explained, which only confused me further.

"Surge?" I asked.

"Yes, we thought it was a diagnostic error at the time, but there was a dramatic uptick in activity along a 96 hour window, roughly Sunday through Wednesday. There was an uptick in stress hormones, and it sent the nanites into overdrive. We are, in short, learning things as we go," he said.

"That's roughly when I got the eviction notice," I announced, as Andropov's face lit up with interest. He began making notes rapidly.

"Fascinating," he replied.

"It's a trial, I know there were risks, how bad is it, am I ok?" My tone conveyed my worry through the collar. .

"It looks like we might be slightly exceeding our upper safety threshold. We're going to keep you for a few days, run some function tests, do more intensive scans and make sure everything is ok. After this, we will dial back some on your booster regimen to balance out the system. Also, we are going to make some changes to your tanking schedule again." He announced, ominously.

"How bad is it?" I asked.

"All will be well, but I remind you again you are a pioneer. We are learning much from you with all the surprises along the way. As such, we will continue to tank you in February, but we are going to go slower, adding at least another month to the process. I want to monitor your changes and make sure we avoid another surge. That will put your emergence roughly, around Halloween." He explained, as I chittered worriedly.

"Eight months? Ok, you're the doctor," I said, my nervousness evident.

"Everything will be fine, but, coming back around to your neural event; you may have some spaciness and greater flexibility issues going forward. I will be direct; there is very little we can do about those if they present themselves." He laid it all out, as if he was ordering a pizza. I recognized the training.

"Thank you doctor, I understand."

"I'll be back in to check on you later," he replied, and left.

"Joyce, how are you feeling?" John asked, as if unleashed by the doctor's absence.

"Fine, kinda hyper... nervous... Hungry," I reported.

"I'm worried about you," he replied.

I chirred and reached out, pulling him down for a hug, as contented noises, a rumbling flowed from my throat.

"It's fine. I can be a little spacey, John, I'm becoming an otter," I reminded him.

"Yeah, but all those talks about not losing yourself, not being first. Don't let your eagerness get you killed, as it were," John chided, in worried tone.

"I know, and as hard as I try to be objective about it, even the scary parts have a kind of joy. I don't want to lose myself. I'm glad they caught it, really glad. I was just a day away from the week booster trip ya know, and who knows what that would have done," I said , assuming that this week's dose was a firm skip.

"Ok. Just, ease back ok? You're my best friend; need you around for when it's my turn." He slipped a card into my right forepaw. The edge caught my paw pad and I twitched; they were getting sensitive in some ways.

Turning it over, it revealed the name of a real estate agent in Kelowna, John's hometown.

"Cabin is going on the market in February. Pulled some money out of savings from my time deployed and have a crew out there fixing it up. Going to buy an old shuttle, put it in storage and when my enlistment is up, join you out there on Centioc. You need to be around for that," he announced.

The tears again. It was a promise, a commitment that I would not be leaving him behind. He was moving slower, but he would join me out there.

A nurse entered and patiently waited for John and I to finish our conversation.

"Going to go down to the cafeteria, want anything?" he asked. I clung to the paper card like it was fine treasure.

"Fish," I replied.

"I might have guessed," he answered and left.

"Name?" The Nurse asked, stepping up as John exited, scanning my bracelet, reading a display.

"Joyce Coswell."

"Date of birth?"

"February 23rd, 2049"

"Do you know where you are right now?" the By 3 awareness check.

"United Earth Medical Center."

"And who is the chancellor of Earth?" she pushed, last question if I got it right.

"Vicki Gomez. I think we can do better." The nurse smiled a sympathetic professional smile, and hung the bag, leaving.

Chapter 13

Function tests they call them.

Try as I might, I could only see them as games.

"Ok, tap the blue squares that pop up on your screen this time," Dr Andropov ordered, over a speaker from another room. I was wearing a sensor cap, outputting to any number of machines.

"Ready to play," I responded eagerly, bouncing in my seat. There was a growing energy to my moment to moment existence that kept me on the edge of everything, always ready to move and engage.

The screen filled with a box that then resolved to large squares of various colors.

I eagerly set to my task.

Hours of this ticked by, not purely digital. One involved stacking cups of all things.

It honestly wasn't a bad way to spend an afternoon.

Finally, exhausted, I was wheeled back to the hospital bed. Dr Andropov entered with a booster bag.

"I thought we were slowing down?" I said, confused, emitting my chirp like bark, softly.

"We are, only one bag this week. Slow down does not mean stop," he grinned, pausing to wink.

"Am I going home soon? I need to pack," I asked. End of the month was approaching and I had to be out in 9 days, coordinate with Ricky, all of that.

"After this bag, in fact. While you are waiting, would you connect your tablet to the hospital server, and log into your patient account? There are some apps you need to download. I'll explain with your discharge package," he said, absently, as he checked the flow for the bag and then left.

Using my tablet was becoming a function test in and of itself, but gradually I managed, only closing the window by accident four times.

Curiosity got the better of me; I had nothing better to do.

There were function tests, like tap the square. More games.

Diving in, it provided ready distraction between the waves of physical symptoms that ebbed and flowed as the treatment drained down into my IV line.

A wave of familiar tiredness threatened to drag me down.

Hmm... must be about an hour and a half in. I thought before the world faded around me.

"Joyce? Joyce?" A heavily accented English again, Dr. Andropov.

My eyes clicked open.

"Yeah?" I acknowledged blearily; my head was pounding, but otherwise, my world was warm and comfortable. An angrier chitter escaped my throat, I wanted to sleep.

"We are about wrapped up here. Your friend is waiting for you down in reception. Is time for discharge, but first, once you've woken up a bit, we will talk a little more about the road going forward." His plans for my non-drowsiness were optimistic at best.

I sat up and willed myself to focus, using the back of my paws to rub the sleep out of my eyes, and then, I groomed some; it was comforting.

The doctor made a few notes on his clipboard that he almost always seemed to carry. It was either that, or he summoned it, by some strange technology.

More than likely, it stayed in a hidden pocket inside his lab coat.

"So I see from the data I'm getting here, that you've already discovered your function tests." The doctor waggled his mysterious digital clipboard and I tracked it eagerly.

"Games," I nodded, and he chuckled.

"You've become very play-oriented. It's interesting to see how your psychology is changing." He pointed out the obvious, but then made a note. He seemed to be enjoying this almost as much as I was.

"Glad to be fun for ya doc," I smiled.

"Yes. Anyhow. At least an hour per day, I do not think that will be a problem though. What we are seeing from your scans the last few days, is that regular stimulation prevents you from falling into certain rhythms that lead to a kind of cascade. An update has been pushed to your bracelet to show your accumulated time," he said, indicating with his right hand.

Tapping it, it showed my time left till my next booster dose, and then another section flashed by

Test = 42.35/60

A happy chirr ensued; I was already ahead.

More notes on the clipboard.

"What do you keep writing down?" I asked, my curiosity surging.

He startled, taken a bit by my directness.

"Sorry," I excused. "Just curious."

"Just notes about your changes. Everything is fine." He made more notes.

A higher pitched bark presented itself, and I blushed under my fur.

Even... more... notes... Gah!

Quickly taking up my tablet, in fumbling paws, I set in on my game and ignored the doctor for a moment.

My world calmed.

"Joyce?" he asked. I looked around, and set down my tablet. The bracelet vibrated. "Ten more minutes... Oooh, almost to goal."

"Joyce?" he said again.

"Sorry, lot going on in my world. Kind of distractible," I answered.

More notes.

Maybe if I took his pen....No... that would be bad.

"Yes, as I said, the neurological changes will persist on some level. You seem to be adapting to them fine though. Keep up with the tests, and we will see you next week. A noise distracted me from the nurse's station, I looked away. When I turned my head back, Dr. Andropov was exiting and the clipboard had vanished from view.

The mystery continued.

Chapter 14

It was Christmas, moving day was three days away.

The apartment was looking barren, and aside from my function games, there was a new hot ticket in town. 'Put the right thing, in the right box.'

It was so simple. Embarrassingly simple, but the fact that it involved a repetitive task that involved hunting objects and being quick, gave me a way to compete with both myself, and John. It was exhausting, but I had kept it up, nosing into cupboards and emptying out drawers.

"That's another one," he teased, inspiring an angry chitter.

"You're wiping the floor with me," I complained.

"Should I go easy on you fluffy?" he continued.

That deserved an angry bark. He got one.

I narrowed my eyes.

"So very fierce," he replied, holding up his hands. The bastard had disarmed me. I blushed under my fur and chirred.

Waddling slowly towards the bedroom, I found a few things we had missed, and completed my set.

"Another for me," I announced with ample pride, and flopped, exhausted.

Without asking, he set a squeezable water bottle nearby; gripping it in both paws, I tilted it up, and carefully swallowed down some water.

"Thank you," I replied. There was a fuzzy feeling followed by a white noise, then my voice collar popped.

"Another outage?" he asked; my ability to use it came and went, but I had it down pretty solid by this point.

'Yes, I think it's down,' I tried to say; failing I looked up at him and nodded.

He used the opportunity to stack the most recent boxes in the ever-filling dining room; we only had a narrow path left to the kitchen.

Focus Joyce. I ordered, then became distracted by a ball of lint that floated by my vision.

Dammit.

Focus...turn on- you "Damn machine." Pay dirt.

"Got it back," I replied.

"Two minutes this time. A new record," he tapped his watch stopping the timer.

Lately, he had been encouraging my playfulness.

My stomach then rumbled; I went to get up, but found that I couldn't. My skeleton felt locked.

From one problem to another.

"If you don't mind, I'm going to lay here a while," I announced.

"Can't move?" He knew me.

"Yep."

There was a knock at the door.

I flailed, trying to move.

"Don't get up, I'll get it." John drifted by effortlessly, and opened the door without a problem.

I remembered when I could do things like that.

Not being able to move always depressed me.

I flailed a bit more; there was a loud pop in my back that caused a wave of pain to race down my legs, sending tingles through my flippers and paws.

Ow. That was stupid.... but at least I could move.

Hail Joyce, master of her domain, conqueror of the jury rigged skeleton.

John finished opening the door just as I managed to stagger myself up with the help of my friend, the couch, revealing Ricky and Sonya. They were wearing Santa hats; Ricky had a number of boxes and a cooler with him.

"Happy holidays." He stepped in with a flourish and executed an unintentionally murderous grin; his smile was made of daggers.

I suppose I was doing a little better these days.

"Guys, but... what... John...." I complained.

"Hey, it can't be work all the time." Ricky shrugged.

Quickly making room on top of a level set of empty boxes, Ricky set down the contents he was carrying, inspiring in me an immediate curiosity.

Ignoring my interest, John set out two folding chairs for our guests, *in front*, of the parcels and they sat, occluding my view.

I chittered in annoyance.

"So the place is coming apart, eh? Movers coming Monday still?" Ricky asked, his form made a series of rhythmic, rapid pops as he sat down, and I saw him wince.

Sonya looked around quietly, before waving awkwardly. "Hi everyone."

"This is a surprise," I said, stating the obvious, trying to start a conversation about something other than boxes.

"Well holidays is about family, and starting a colony together seems to rank up there. Not too many days left to celebrate before we are packing up to go. Last Christmas before the tank." Ricky had a point. Next Christmas I would be almost two months out. I would be an *otter*.

The idea excited me.

"Anyone else want a beer?" John rose, and fished one out of the refrigerator, carefully navigating around the moving inspired maze that was occupying more and more of the open floor space.

"Hey man, quit reading my mind, wait for the movie," Ricky complained, and then flexed a paw, his retractable claws briefly popping up.

Sonya just shook her head. Her changes, at least personality-wise had been the most dramatic. A few months ago, she was on the verge of being nosy; she was a tax lawyer, and doing most of the colonies' accounting.

There was a fire, an assertiveness to her that had now faded some; she was practically hiding behind Ricky.

"Water... please, If that's ok." Folding her paws, putting them in her lap, she looked down at the floor.

"Heavy drinker, coming out," John intoned with a joke.

Bright, happy fun holiday times. I forgot about the boxes.

116

"So, have you heard?" Ricky flashed a grin.

"Heard what? Is everything ok?" My panic quickly jumped. The only time things were newsworthy anymore was when things were on fire.

I preferred my cartoons. In that world, cats could recover from falling anvil hits. There had been another murder of a morphic just last week. They had been slated to be in the second half of the first five hundred.

I only caught the headline. In truth, I already knew the story.

Pain was always something humans liked to inflict on what they didn't understand.

"Easy, relax. I was up at the ship, in boneyard Gemini. Oh she's pretty, reminds me of my days as a cadet." He took a pull off his beer, and I saw John grow more interested.

"You were a cadet on a Gen 1?" John asked and Ricky laughed.

Sonya and I shared a look. *Here we go.*

"Oh yeah man, back in the cowboy days. Fission initiators and everything, seat of your pants. Shit breaking left and right. People don't realize how bootstrapped the first fifty were. Once they had to take the Hammerhead down for a retrofit, those BEC-2 upgrades... God what a fucking nightmare," he complained, nostalgically. His eyes sparkled as he remembered the past.

"Sounds like you miss it," John commented. The statement made no sense to me, but Ricky nodded, eagerly.

"Every day. Looking forward to getting back out there. My last deep space trip, hauling us fuzzies to our new home." He took another long pull, and his eyes took on a far look.

"You say that, but I still have to get the taxes filed, and the regulations worked out with UEA treasury for the tax schedule, or we are going to have a real issue going forward into the next fiscal year," Sonya mentioned, in apparent Greek.

We all blinked, flabbergasted, and she briefly pulled away from the conversation.

"That's what we have you for. I'm the mechanical engineer, you are the financial engineer," he chuckled.

As if some hidden signal was sent, John rose and began moving boxes into the kitchen, except for the cooler.

"A Christmas feast, made for fuzzies," Ricky announced, finally setting the cooler down in front of me. My eyes danced in revelry at what it might contain within, and I barked eagerly doing everything I could to restrain my curiosity.

"Ricky, I think I love you," John called out, removing two thick steaks from a box.

"One of those is for me. Don't get greedy," Ricky chided.

Sonya quietly picked her way into a kitchen and found a pear in a box, with a few cans of Bamboos shoots.

Letting the men do the kitchen work, we fell back and watched.

"Should we be recording this?" she asked, showing signs of life beyond tax code.

"It's a brave new world, and everything is changing." We shared a conspiratorial giggle.

John pulled out a pan from under the cabinet, which made a cacophonous noise and hurt my ears.

"Don't burn mine, I like it rare," Ricky micromanaged.

"You remind me of a sergeant I had in Basic, always riding my ass," John replied, in playful banter.

Military men.

"Joyce, are you going to open yours?" Ricky asked, and John looked up with a grin.

My focus immediately re-centered from of the drama in the kitchen to the plastic mystery in front of me. I was teeming with curiosity and excitement.

Drawing closer, a clinging smell around the cooler sent lightning flashes through my brain, an excited grunt followed as I opened it and the rest of the smells washed over me.

Trout filets and mussels.

Real mussels!

An explosion of happy, if feral noises, exploded from my throat in a volcanic eruption of chittering, clicking and chirping.

Everyone laughed.

One hour later, we could all barely move, having eaten our weight in food.

Sonya was still going, determined to eat double her weight in bamboo shoots, while Ricky made a low guttural, almost meowing growl, holding his stomach.

"Really glad it's not one of the sick days," he remarked absently. The two other actively shifting morphics in the room, Sonya and I, nodded eagerly, agreeing with his assessment.

"Too good of a meal to lose," John added, sprawled out on the couch.

"A swim would be nice," I commented absently, thoughts drifting to the lapping of waves against my back, in a comfortable sea, as I idly played with some empty mussel shells still remaining on my chest.

"You know, what's stopping us? This place has a hot tub doesn't it?" John asked the room.

I had been afraid of my community since the angry notice about the colony meeting. Being evicted hadn't helped either, so I had become a ghost, barely leaving my apartment.

This felt like defiant rebellion. Almost as if I was throwing a Molotov of my own through the front office.

"I don't know," Sonya volunteered, sounding as unsure as I felt, as she finished off another can of the shoots.

"What's the harm? You're a paying tenant, there's no rule against it; you are out of here Monday, and its going to be empty because of the holidays. Frankly Joyce, fuck 'em. You have every right," John said, defiance burning in his voice.

"He is technically correct." Sonya checked in, legal training evident.

"Still, what about Ricky?" I was running out of excuses, and it did seem like a great idea.

"You're thinking house cats, sweet heart. Ocelots are swimmers. Who do you think caught that trout you inhaled?" He flashed a grin. "Was a fisherman before, I'm a fisher cat now."

John disappeared and returned with a number of draw string shorts and black T-shirts.

"Five years in the military. Every event has some kind of free shirt." John and Ricky were roughly the same size, but Ricky, was a little more squat and stocky.

"Come on Sonya, let's see what we can find," I offered, and she eagerly joined me.

Ten minutes later and we all looked as if we had been part of some kind of gym rat apocalypse. Black Central Command fun run; half-marathon shirts hung large from the diminutive frames of Sonya and myself hiding the shorts we were wearing, evident only by the long draw strings that went down almost to the floor.

John and Ricky looked much more normal, minus the fact that Ricky had the fur and markings of an ocelot, and retractable claws on both his hands and hind paws.

The Dolphin Bay preferred to bill itself as a "Luxury Rental Experience." This meant it had a closet for a gym, and a "spa room" consisting of a large hot tub and heated pool. They were fine luxuries, if they weren't intended to be used by a community of seven hundred people.

Four years, and I had seldom used the amenities I had paid all the extra rent for. Hot Tubs are less fun when they are filled with strangers.

My hind flippers slapped noisily against the concrete, I wasn't wearing shoes. There was little point, and then, I slipped into the water of the heated pool.

My fur, and the oils on it, though incomplete, were keeping me partially dry. Then something kicked in; my body relaxed. I flipped over on my back and floated.

It was *rapturous*

"I think we've lost the otter," I heard Ricky mention distantly.

Why hadn't I done this before?

A half hour of warm inky blackness descended, buoyed on the edges by the sounds of distant conversations coming from the hot tub.

"Joyce?" I perked up and thrashed over in the water, and swam over to the edge of the pool. It was much easier to move, and I reveled in the freedom.

"Yeah?"

"Going to join us over here or swim by yourself all night?" John asked. I was torn, but why not.

Pulling myself out, my body sagged and protested against the weight, but it was short lived. I could float all I wanted later.

My friends had helped me find my courage and face my fears; now they just wanted to spend time with me.

Fair trade.

John scooted to make more room in the hot tub, bumping into Sonya.

I splashed in. They say if you give an otter a thimbleful of water, they can soak a room. This, was my legacy.

"Hey fish breath," he said as he pushed some water at me; I chittered in defiance.

Muscles uncorked from tension, and I felt another nap threatening to come on.

"So John, when do you deploy out?" Sonya asked, elements of her curiosity still showing through her new shyness.

"On the 3rd. Going to see Aqua Girl here off on Monday and then head up to the cabin in Kelowna, a few days, sort some things out." The news of the Danube going in for retrofit was all over the place; his orders were hardly classified. She was in the first group of Gate-capable ships.

They were going to be our escort out to Centioc. The First Contact team ferrying the first morphics to Centioc One.

John reported to me in confidence that the Mendians had ate it up.

Suddenly, two people walked into the pool room.

The woman screamed, the man dropped his keys. Scurrying back, they slowly made their way out.

"Oh shit," Ricky said, looking around.

"Let's stay," John insisted, spoiling for a fight.

A nervous bark escaped my throat, and I chirped a bit, distressed, looking around.

That's when I noticed the surveillance camera was broken. It was a serious safety issue, but it also made way for an opportunity.

An idea hit.

"No let's vanish. Hide. Sneak back to the apartment. Let's mess with their heads," I urged, gesturing to the broken camera. Our window was closing; they could be calling security, but the side exit lets out to the parking lot. It could work!

"If we aren't here, we can deny," chimed Sonya, being the legal eagle...red panda, got it.

"Exactly. I dunno what they're talking about. They're nuts, we've been here all night. How many people do you need for a solid alibi?" I asked Sonya.

"Trial law is not my area, but two," she replied.

John flashed that wicked grin; it matched the daggers showing from Ricky's smile.

The two military men moved according to their training and, in seconds, were ready to go.

Sonya and I anchored them and risked it all, but we held.

Looping back through the shuttle parking lot, we cut a wide arc, and quietly re-entered the apartment through the patio door, then set up the screen with a casual family game. The scattered plates and glasses left over from dinner provided ample evidence we had spent the evening in.

An hour passed. Quick showers ensued, and I was out of towels and dish rags for all the fur we had to collectively dry. John had to use one of his fun-run shirts.

He drew the short straw, having only skin to worry about.

Nervously, I watched the clock. An hour and twenty minutes ticked by.

A sharp angry knock rocketed through the apartment.

It was Clark, the building manager, flanked by two security guards.

"Got a complaint you were at the pool," he announced without preamble.

"Nope, been here all night," I flatly denied. His eyes narrowed on me.

"And even if she hadn't, might I inquire how it would be against the rules?" Sonya rose, finding a shaky confidence.

"And you are?" He stiffened up, trying to intimidate her.

She flinched, but held. "My name is Sonya Richards, *Esquire*, Attorney at Law." The words hung in the air with all the indications of a threat as she handed over her card.

He looked at it, then around the room, and grumbled, the air quickly deflating from his jackboot bravado.

"Never mind. Be out by the end of the month." He turned and walked off.

I slammed the door behind him and we all waited a moment for him to walk away, eyeing each other conspiratorially.

Then the dam broke, with Ricky losing it first.

"Oh my God, did you see the look on his face?" He yowled, in between high arcing fits of screeching laughter.

"Best Actor Award has to go to Sonya Richards, *Esquire,* Attorney at Law. That was fucking brilliant, you might as well have kicked him in the balls," John commented, and even though her skin was hidden by fur, I could tell Sonya was blushing.

"Everyone fears lawyers." Sonya flashed a grin, her eyes shone with pride.

"So, let's keep the party going," Ricky commented, as John tossed him another beer.

Chapter 15

It was moving day. Everything was sore. I attempted to slide off the air mattress and I couldn't

"John?" I called out.

Silence.

"Anyone here?" Hoping for Ricky or Sonya.

Nobody.

Shit.

A white flash of pain erupted from behind my eyes and then a familiar pop was heard from my voice collar.

Double shit.

A tense chirping bark followed. Everything *hurt.* Yesterday, I had seriously overdone it with the packing.

I needed to pee. Willing my legs to move, or more so my flippers to respond, they only twitched. I could feel them, but my skeleton was locked.

This did not feel like a game. This was not fun. I was 'trapped, desperate.'

Finally, I flipped myself over, and dragged myself by my forepaws into the bathroom and made it to the tub. It was undignified, and terrible.

I could still cry, I discovered.

Midway through a very awkward shower, something cracked, and it made me scream in pain. My world sparkled and my chest heaved with endorphins as everything got heady from the rush of it all.

Finally, I could move my hind quarters again.

Shaking and unsteady, I got myself pulled up and cleaned off. Hobbling very slowly, every movement was an agony and although famished, I did not have the energy to think about eating.

Couch and cartoons... Save me sweet canary.

Flopping onto the couch with all the grace and trajectory of a tumbling spacecraft, my skeleton protested angrily, rewarding me with more pain, before sliding into an uneasy comfort.

Why was I doing this to myself?

The question offended me; the idea that even part of me could question, would question. An angry chitter escaped my throat.

No... Fuck off brain... This is my dream...

It was a bad morning, a very, very bad morning, and I was alone.

More tears. *Dammit! Stop!*

A familiar sense of anger and self-hatred like an old friend, sat down at the edge of the couch with me. Setting its pitchfork down on the table, I could almost see its demonic grin as it leaned over me with a diabolical sneer.

Didn't think you'd be rid of me that easily, did you?

Vaudevillian laughter. It snapped me out of my day dream.

The cat on the screen was considering making a deal for its soul, with a cartoon devil.

I skipped to the next one in the queue.

My stomach rumbled, as hunger won the battle over lethargy. Straining, I went to get up, only to find that my skeleton was locked again, my range of motion limited.

More crawling, dragging myself by my forepaws across the floor and then back again, the day intent on putting me through my paces.

Falling asleep on the way, I eventually woke up in even greater pain to find John kneeling over me worriedly.

"Joyce, are you ok?" Ricky and Sonya were standing in the door, with grocery bags. I saw John had his tablet in hand ready to dial emergency service.

'I'm fine. No, I'm not fine, but I'm stable, medically,' I quickly explained through my non-working voice collar.

.... Fuck... I nodded, indicating I was ok, but then cried.

"I'm sorry I wasn't here," he said as he held me. It hurt, I didn't care.

A squelched yelp followed as he lifted me gently and got me set on the couch.

"Do you need the doctor?" he asked. Ricky and Sonya quietly slipped in and set down the bags.

"Hey trooper, feeling bad?" Ricky asked.

Sonya chirred worriedly.

My friends surrounding me was the first bright light of my morning, the feeling of family.

I held up my fore paw and waggled it.

"Voice collar is out I take it," Sonya asked, and I chirped, nodding in confirmation.

The apartment became a flurry of activity as Ricky, Sonya and John worked to set me up.

A can of tuna and a few gulps of water later and my mood was steadily improving.

Focus on the words, push them to the collar. *You... stupid... damn...* "Machine".

Everyone looked over at me.

"Finally." It had been hours, a weight lifted off of me.

"It's been a bad day," I reported; it felt good to finally be able to get that out.

"Booster. Booster." My wrist device vibrated.

Ugh...

"Don't move, I'll get it," John announced, loading the dose carefully and bringing it to me.

It activated and I shot-gunned it down.

The morning began to arc vaguely up, then the movers came.

Everyone exploded into activity, except for me. I couldn't move my hind flippers and was stuck on the couch.

Everyone helped as the boxes emptied and the apartment grew more sparse by the moment.

Again, except for me; even trying to get up had inspired a 15 minute nap.

Frustrated chitters. Deep vexation. This awful day, existing as a figurehead at the center of my life.

An observer, not a participant.

The newness had worn off; I was accustomed to difference. Now there were just the consequences, and the cost laid bare. No excitement, no overwhelming joy. My forepaws were common; my fur, every day.

But now I couldn't move. Couldn't help. Couldn't participate.

God Dammit. This sucked.

More frustrated noises, sounding more like an animal than anything. That thought brought a warm feeling of joy, confirming this was no question of identity. There was no regret of the program in that moment. It was the frustration at the cost.

I wanted it to be *over*, but how much easier was life going to be as a quadruped?

There was nothing better to do, but watch my friends and the hired laborers do my work for me, so I dove into the introspection, feeling no need even for games.

This was no time for play. I hurt.

Even my canary abandoned me, as the apartment emptied around.

They had to take the screen at some point.

Finally, as I looked sullenly out through the sliding glass door at the beautiful sunshine-filled day outside, brooding over my predicament, John approached.

"You're the last thing to pack," he mentioned, trying for levity, instead stabbing me, unknowingly, right where it hurt.

"I can't walk right now. I don't know what to do." I broke down in tears; he knelt and comforted me.

"Feel so goddamned useless right now." Every part of me was trembling with shame and despair. All I wanted to do was sleep.

"It's ok, you're sick and it's making everything terrible. Hang in there, Aqua Girl, you're tough." It was the second time he had used that nickname. I smiled in spite of myself.

"Don't feel so tough," I replied, sullenly.

"That's the only time it shows. It's not about what's easy..." he began, it was an old saying of ours; it had gotten us through many nights and I knew it well.

"It's about what's right," I replied, and my conviction firmed up underneath me.

The hard truth of it, looking deep within, considering all of the challenges ahead and behind me...

"I'm becoming an otter," I said simply.

"Yes you are, and no matter how hard it gets, you've got people to get you through it," John replied.

134

He and Ricky carried me, with the couch to the base of the rusted shuttle and then gently transferred me on board.

Chapter 16

Snow was everywhere. Mt. Shasta imposed greatly on the skyline, dwarfing the three bedroom cabin that perched on 5 partially cleared acres that belonged to Ricky.

His retirement retreat.

It was private, and quiet, everything I needed in my last few weeks before the tank. John was back on the Danube and firmly out of contact, but I had been almost too busy to miss him.

I would soon be sleeping for seven months, and then, shortly after, moving to a new planet.

Wheelchair bound, and hurting terribly, there was still so much left to do.

"Ow!" A plaintive whine escaped Sonya's mouth as she gripped her right forepaw, dropping the pen she was holding. Her fingers were much more clubbed, and dexterity was becoming harder for her. Still, she was light years ahead of me and so she had been filling out the forms.

Over the last two weeks, I had watched the quality of her handwriting degrade from lawyer, to medical doctor.

Still, the best I could do anymore with a pen- approached pre-school; she firmly had me beat.

"Yeah, I think I'm done for the night," she announced. It was 9 in the morning, which made for the end of her day. She and Ricky both were nocturnal by species and preference, leaving me with quiet afternoons to myself.

The two shifts meant that the work never really had to stop though, and plans for the colony were moving apace.

"I think we are going to make it at this rate. Knock off for the day," I commented, tapping through a digital form on my tablet, carefully.

Accessibility features made it easier, making some things bigger, and easier to target with my paw pads.

It was like a more difficult function test.

My entire life had become a more difficult function test.

"Booster. Booster." Sonya's bracelet went off, startling her. She startled easily more and more lately. It was strange. There was a preeminent focus to her that could be shattered in a dramatic instant.

I checked mine out of habit as she left the room, and realized I was behind in my tests for the Doctor. *Another thing to keep up with.*

Watch me juggle, watch me dance. I twitched a flipper trying to move my hips to no result.

Ok, maybe dancing was out, but I could still juggle.

My tablet tumbled out of my paws as if in defiance of any remaining confidence of my ability to function, sliding firmly out of reach.

Shit.

I barked at it in anger, feeling frustrated. Sonya poked her head out of the kitchen.

"Problem?" she asked with a yawn. I heard the click of the device on the counter, and could distantly smell the chalky looking liquid's artificial scent.

Plastic human spy juice. I was very tired of it.

Two weeks to tank. Just two more weeks and I'd be done.

Ricky walked in with two more filets, yawning. The cabin was suddenly a bustling center of activity.

"I dropped my tablet." Ricky and Sonya both scanned the floor and found it, handing it back to me, as Sonya's rang; she quickly excused herself to take it.

"Breakfast?" he offered, handing me one of them, a beautifully cut filet of fish steak.

I devoured it, raw, I did not care.

"I'll take that as a yes." Ricky watched on in amazement, taking the other and began breading and frying it.

Part of me felt like he was ruining it.

A series of panicked noises erupted from Sonya's bedroom, and she exploded forward back into the living in a flurry of activity.

"Shit shit shit." She was freaking out.

Then she fell over, almost fainting.

"Easy, remember how it is when you panic," I reminded her, and she began to breath deeper.

We had been getting a lot of practice in the last few weeks.

"Big... Problem," she gasped out.

"Regional office... lost a form... Couldn't find me. License is up in the air," she rattled off.

"Shit... That is bad." I said.

Her breathing spiked briefly up; showing clearly my blunder.

"What does that mean?" Ricky asked. I heard the cooking filet flip in the pan. My mouth watered.

Ruined or not, I wanted some.

"If I don't have a license, we have to find someone else to do the forms, already on a shoestring. *Fucked.*"

"Ok. Ok, that's what could happen, how do we keep it from happening?" They were both tired and at the end of their day; it was keeping us from solutions and focusing only on the problem.

"I can fill out the forms, but I need to get them in tonight. Buddy of mine in processing can rush them through," she replied, her panic again rising.

I got it.

"You're about to twelve , aren't you?" It was an unwritten law of the shifting process it seemed, that after twelve hours awake, you were normally down for twelve to eighteen. It was just the way it worked, and you could set your watch by it.

She nodded. "Already feeling it. Hard to focus, and fatigued."

"Ricky?" I asked, seeking options.

"Within an hour or two of the same," he replied, leaving it up to me.

I chittered, turning it over in my head.

"If you fill out the forms, and I brought them down to the regional office in Los Angeles, would that fix this?" I asked.

"How would we get you there?" Ricky asked.

That did present a problem.

"What about a private shuttle service? It's expensive but not nearly as much as paying a tax attorney. Not to mention we don't have the time to look. We could take it out of the discretionary fund." It was a dwindling resource, at best, but this was an emergency.

Sonya jabbed at her tablet, obviously entering numbers and working it out with a sigh.

"I hate to say it, but it's our best option. Still, LA, alone, in your state?" Her worry was evident.

"This thing rolls on its own when I push the stick, so all I really have to do is sit here, and deliver papers. Should be easy." A worry went through me as I said it. *Famous last words?*

"Ok. I'll make the arrangements," Sonya surrendered to my logic, wearily.

Ricky plopped down with his half of the trout filet and began to dive in; he cut off a quarter, and offered it to me.

I devoured it, feeling, as always, hungry.

"Thanks for doing all of this," he said.

"We're a family Ricky. This has us all tied together. I've got a place to sleep and fish to eat because of you," I reminded him and he simply nodded.

"Yeah, still. If it's not one thing it's another. News is getting bad all the time. It's eating at me, ya know? The ugliness. I want to get out there where it's clean, leave it all behind. Start over, away from all the stuff that's holding us *back*." He took a drink of water from a glass, and set it on the table, and he paused, reflective.

"Remember, we are getting out. Eventually they are going to run out of hoops. It's inevitable. We have the ship, we have the people and we have the will. We're gonna make it Ricky. Just think, in ten years, Centioc might be the place to shift; a world where people go to be *free.*" It was hard not to feel utopian about the future. As the world grew more ugly, the colony committee was drawing together tighter and tighter.

Pioneers, far from the sins of our forefathers, striking out onto the new frontier.

Sonya reemerged, looking half dead from fatigue, holding a manilla packet.

"The shuttle is ours for the day, and will be here in an hour. I wrote the instructions on the front of the packet and I'll go sleep now. Thank you," she announced, without further ceremony or preamble, dragging herself heavily towards her bedroom.

"Screen?" Ricky offered.

"Sure," I agreed.

He turned on the news. *Bleh.*

Time to catch up on function tests.

A notification popped up on my tablet.

"*Private Transport arriving in 48 minutes*.*

Spiffy.

Find the blue square... one of my favorites...

Protests continue in continental capitals and regional centers over the Treaty of Gates and the passage of funding in UEA parliament for the opening of one hundred and fifty new shifting clinics, part of phase one implementation following completion of the first half of the Morphic Beta Program, in November.

They were talking about us! A bit of pride rushed through me as the screen lit up red and the tablet vibrated. I had missed something...

Damn distractions.

Ricky had fallen asleep on the couch, curled up, head resting on his hand paws.

Quietly, I reached over and turned off the screen and pushed the stick to move me outside, and wait for transport.

With my hoodie, and under the blanket, I could truly enjoy the beauty of the snow. My fur was getting quite thick, and seemed to be fully in over my face, which was a boon in this colder climate.

I could feel the weather through it, distantly, but overall, I was content and comfortable.

Finishing the math part of the tests, simple arithmetic and multiplication, I checked my time.

Forty-five minutes for the day; I was nearing my goal, but that also meant my shuttle would be arriving soon.

A black, shiny, executive shuttle drifted down from the sky, alighting gracefully in the yard, a stunning juxtaposition to Ricky's ancient rusted craft. It was boxy, but it had a glossy obsidian finish, even its windows were tinted. The pilot, in a suit, jogged down the ramp, confirmed he was there for me and wheeled me up with hardly a word.

Sonya had gone a little overboard in making certain I would be ok.

"Alright Miss. Is there anything I can get you, champagne for the trip or perhaps water, caviar?" he offered.

"Caviar?" How much had she spent? I desperately wanted to try some, but feared what all this was costing.

Guilt got the better of me.

"Just water for now thanks, but could you loosen the cap?" It was embarrassing to rely so much on a stranger, but he seemed eager to attend to every demand.

"No problem at all, miss," he replied and handed it over.

"What's your name? I'm Joyce, Joyce Coswell, you don't need to be so formal. I'm kind of overwhelmed by all of this," I admitted. I was a simple nurse, and a simple otter.

"I'm Kareem, Kareem Ali. Pleasure to make your acquaintance," he offered his hand, and I offered my paw.

He took it graciously and shook it. It felt good to know there were still humans in the world that weren't afraid of us.

"Excuse me a moment."

"This is execucar-1078 requesting guidance information for flight path into Los Angles on the 5 Memorial Skyway."

"Roger that. Proceed to coordinates and execute path. Safe flight." Flight control kicked off.

"Thirty minutes to LA miss..." he replied.

The craft lifted off and I watched out of my large tinted window, which took up much of one side of the craft. Once we hit a certain altitude, the craft turned.

"We are at 3500 meters and on our way to LA," Kareem Announced, "By the way, do you know why they call this skyline the memorial 5?"

"No, but I'd love to know." The conversation was keeping my mind off my anxiety of being in LA alone; it was a wretched hive, regardless of its international prestige.

In a world of gleaming golden cities, Los Angeles was pyrite, as fake and manufactured as the film industry that was once based there.

"Back in the age of nations, that road you can see below us was something called an interstate. Was a trade and military thing. The I5 was its name," he offered.

That was interesting.

"Why was it called the 5? Not the 1 or the 672 or something?" I pushed.

He shrugged. "I dunno, still, it's a fun bit of trivia." The highway below stretched out to the horizon like a ribbon. They were mainly used by the drone haulers for shipping goods and local access. Shuttles were so much faster and ubiquitous, much better for distant travel.

The LA skyline began to become visible. Rows of impossibly tall skyscrapers dotted the landscape, most with large platforms radiating out from their top decks, in rows of two or three.

Shuttle parking.

The craft began to angle for one of them, pitching low. It appeared for a moment we were heading right for the building, but gradually a black space resolved out of the greater picture, as the shuttle glided into a large bay, coming to rest in a pad, for shuttles of its service.

"Alright Miss Coswell, I'll be right here waiting for you," he announced, flicking buttons and lowering the ramp.

Rolling myself down it, I navigated to the elevator without much effort. All of these buildings were designed with accessibility access in mind, and not having to move was saving me a lot of energy.

I had been up the entire thirty minute trip into LA, after a full breakfast.

Watch out world, here I come.

Everything was smooth sailing as I rolled up to the secured area and emptied my pockets, surrendering my tablet, and my headphones- having nothing else.

"Miss, can you remove your bracelet, and put your... hand? on the console?" The security officer asked politely.

"I can't remove the bracelet, it's medical, and locked on, but it serves as my ID." He raised a suspicious eyebrow; I scanned my bracelet, not my hand, and he rose.

"You need to follow my instructions miss or I'm going to need to notify a supervisor," he threatened.

"I'm trying, I'm a morphic; my code is in flux and, thus, the system won't read my G.A.N properly. I'm under the care of Dr. Andropov, United Earth Medical, I'm just here to drop of forms," I explained.

He rose, roughly grabbed my paw, and held it down to the scanner.

"Anomaly detected" flashed in red over the screen.

"What the fuck is going on here?" the guard replied, ignoring my words, growing more panicked.

"Supervisor, I need a supervisor and backup in here right now. Code T3." Everything appeared calm, but then I heard the doors in front of me seal, and lock.

Then the elevators sealed and locked. Save for one, from which a security team soon erupted out of.

Shit.

I was wheeled off into an interview room. Then it got worse.

"Please stop. You're hurting me," I begged. One security guard was holding me up, my skeleton screaming, while another patted me down.

It was only the "Property Of ECC, Do Not Remove" Label inscribed into my bracelet that prevented its removal.

This had become a nightmare.

Mercifully, they sat me back down in my chair, roughly, my frame popped like it was part xylophone.

Then they took my voice collar.

"We'd like you to answer some questions." A supervisor sat down, behind a table in the small interview room I was in.

I chirped angrily, and gestured towards the collar.

"You need to speak up," he said. I gestured more towards the collar.

He finally got it.

"You need that to talk?" he puzzled, gesturing to it.

I chirped in confirmation, nodding.

"Ok..." He replied hesitantly, sliding it, with shaking hand over towards me.

Trembling, with fumbling paws, I slid it on. It took far longer than it should have with my limited dexterity, and terror making my paws numb. Finally I heard the latch click.

Focus on connecting, don't "curse".

"Excuse me?"

"Sorry, it takes a moment to connect, I have to focus," I replied.

"So what the heck is going on here, you're one of those mixers right?" He asked using the more offensive slang.

"Morphic is the preferred term. I'm in the first 250, under the Care of Dr. Andropov. My name is Joyce Coswell," I repeated. My heart was racing, and this was wearing me out. Still I didn't have the luxury of being sick at the moment.

Please, whoever is up there watching over me, let me get through this.

I couldn't imagine what it would be like if they decided to hold me.

"Why didn't you explain this to the officer at the checkpoint?" he demanded.

"I did, all due respect. I explained my code was in shift and that my bracelet worked as my ID. Gave him my doctor's name; he said something about T3 and the next thing I know, I'm here. I was dropping off the forms you took for my lawyer friend." I name dropped Sonya, casually.

He coughed, a part of him went a little white at the mention of an attorney. She was right. People did fear lawyers.

Something John taught me once went through my head. *Perceived power, is achieved power.*

"I'll just slip out and make some calls to United Earth Medical, shouldn't be long." he replied, and excused himself.

Forty-five minutes ticked by. Nervousness ate at me.

Finally, he re-emerged, with my tablet, headphones and packet.

"Very sorry for the mix-up. Let me just finish up this form and you'll be free to go." He rapidly scribbled upon a blue sheet of paper that said "Release of Suspect" on top of it.

I felt as if I had definitely earned my caviar, making a mental note to try it on the way home.

"Would you point me to the right department?" I asked.

"No Ma'am, we can't let you back into the secure area, but I'll deliver your packet. Who's it going to?" he offered, as a type of compromise.

This made no sense.

"I'm sorry but it's rather important I give it to him directly. He's waiting on this. It's essential." I couldn't just hand this off to some nameless person.

"Look," he said, pausing with a sigh. "Your story checks out. Dr. Andropov confirmed everything, identified your bracelet as military tech, but I can't let you back there," he said, mysteriously.

"What is this? What's going on?" I demanded.

"It's from higher up. That's all I can say. Without a working GAN, regardless of your ID Bracelet, I can't clear you through security."

"I have rights. I'm a UEA citizen dammit, I deserve access to my officials. This guy is a bureaucrat in a department, not a tech on a defense platform," I argued.

"Look, stay calm, please, I don't want this to escalate. Seriously miss, I'm on your side, but not everyone here *is*." His voice dropped to a low, conspiratorial whisper.

"My commander is ready to throw your ass in holding and lose your paperwork for 72 hours if you know what I mean. The only reason you aren't right now is Dr. Andropov. I don't want the trouble, so how about you do us both a favor, trust me to get your packet to the gentleman and get out of here before we both have a pain in the ass we don't want to deal with." His tone was urgent and insistent. It was clear he didn't give a shit about me.

"Compromise. Call him, have him meet me down here, I'll hand it off and be gone within half an hour." This way, I could at least see the transfer.

He paused, considering it, looking toward the obvious two-way mirror in the back.

"Deal," he replied, and disappeared to make the arrangements.

It was a simple matter. A nervous looking man wearing a button down dress shirt and black pants appeared. Your typical, generic govt. bureaucrat, about 5'7 and in his early 30s.

"Thanks for going to all the trouble," he said.

"No problem at all," I lied.

"Tell Sonya Hi for me," he replied, and quickly left.

I had an armed escort back to my transport.

It was just another reason to hate LA.

Chapter 17

"Man, forget this planet," Ricky said, dismissively, by the firelight. We were out under the stars on the moon lit night. I was nearing my twelve, but they were just getting started.

I had been catching them up on the adventures of the day.

"I tried the caviar on the way home," I admitted

"So how was it?" Sonya asked.

"I liked the Trout better. Kind of salty." It just didn't hit the right notes for me.

"It's an acquired taste for humans too, I wonder if I'd still like it."

"Who knows, the only thing I really want is meat anymore, and lots of things upset my stomach," Ricky admitted.

"I'm not too much different," I replied.

"Never going to forget watching you scarf down the trout raw. You're a wild animal," he teased.

"Pretty close actually," I admitted.

"Wasn't that kind of the point?" Sonya asked the crowd.

"Nah, you're wrong there. It's about being what you are. I know what they told us about neural imprinting, and all that, but it's more than that... it's not just some clinical thing. This is real, ya know?" Ricky replied, trying to find the words.

"It's like when I look in the mirror... don't really recognize myself anymore, but I do at the same time... Every day the mask eats away a little bit more, almost as if it's getting harder to hide, like the bots are shining a light on me that I can't escape from. No more lies, or shadows," Sonya mused, staring into the fire.

"It's gotten kind of boring for me. I know I'm changing, can't ignore it, but that's been my life for months now; lately, I can't help but look beyond. A chance to start over, on a new world, clean slate. *Free.*" The emotions surged in me.

My fur remained dry. Emotional chirps and chitters escaped my throat; a whimpering chirr followed, but no tears.

Another link in the chains of my humanity had fallen away. The last shadows of my curse were fading.

Gratitude, firm and deep, that it was now, that this was my time- surged through my being.

In that moment, I yearned for the tank. That last step. The final bits of my curse broken as I drifted, silently reforming, moving towards my now inevitable destiny.

154

I snuggled down into my warm blanket with the idea, and sleepily enjoyed the fire.

"You know, out there, a thirteen month year," Ricky volunteered. I nodded in agreement with his facts. "Asteroid moon too, not round like ours."

"It's going to be quiet. I'm looking forward to the quiet," Sonya reported. The latest probe report showed that Centioc had nothing but plant life, a strange blue-green world, mostly forest, with low mountains and even lower seismicity.

It had oceans though, places to swim. There was a whole new planet to discover, and explore.

What awaited me in its depths?

My mind danced with possibilities.

Something twitched... my left flipper cramped, and a guttural throaty growl rumbled.

"You ok?" Sonya checked in.

"Yeah, I think so...." A muscle tensed high in my hip, then cramped, then tore.

There was a muffled pop that caused Ricky and Sonya to both leap to their feet and regard each other worriedly.

I screamed. An animalistic screeching growl wailed out of my throat as my world sprung into patterns of agony.

Distantly, in concert with my screams, I heard a wailing tone, as my left paw vibrated. "Danger. Danger," my wrist bracelet reported.

Everything got woozy as the endorphins hit; my world drifted in and out in burning tortured agonies of awareness.

"Panda. Go bag," Ricky snapped, and Sonya darted off.

I was moving, then vaguely up. Someone carrying me?

Another twitch... a desperate howling yowl. Oh gods, was I dying? What was this...?

Please... make it stop, for the love of whatever is out there, make it stop.

"How is she?" Sonya charged up the ramp, out of breath; she leaned, woozy herself.

"Strap in," Ricky ordered. "I just saw her skull *move.* Something isn't right... We have to get her to the med center. Mayday mayday, this is civilian transport Hell Cat requesting priority vectoring and guidance for Emergency Medical Transport. United Earth Medical Center."

"Request received Hell Cat... Verifying flight credential..."

"Lt Commander, your credentials have been confirmed. Scramble launch is authorized, emergency path has been pushed to your guidance. Safe flight and good luck."

"Sweethearts... This is going to be some cowboy shit... Hold on." Though panicked, there was a pleased sort of tone to his urgency.

An intense feeling of G's as the craft rapidly gained altitude; it hurt, but it simply added it to the chorus.

Sonya screamed... briefly, then she passed out.

Another twinge of high searing agony sent a desperate chittering growl again through my throat as the process repeated with my other hind leg.

Why wouldn't I pass out? White flashes, again, and again and again heralding an ever increasing choir of agony. I howled in pain until my throat felt raw.

In waves it came, all the way to the medical center. He landed and the ramp dropped; before I knew it, Andropov was onboard.

"Relax my little *vydra*. All will be ok now." There was a pin prick in my left arm, and then... I was still awake, but everything was dreamy... kind of hazy.

The fire got distant.

This just got *fun.*

"Hi doc. I think I love you," I reported.

The yellow canary flitted down and alighted upon the edge of the shuttle.

"Where's the kitty?" I asked.

The scene shifted. A chromatic flash of colors and lights. Kaleidoscope parades of prismatic loveliness.

A room... a series of beeps. That strange Russian accent.

Andropov...

a scent...new.. man..

"Dr. Miller, I'm certain you will agree we need to tank now. We have waited far too long," Andropov insisted.

This couldn't be tank day, it was weeks away.

Still, it was a happy dream.

"I warned them about dragging it out like this. Two months, no more... Three with her architecture. Look at these spikes... you put her in a wheelchair?" He was criticizing my friend; it made me vaguely angry.

"My hands were tied. I've made the same arguments, but Central Command gave me the same reply over and over. She signed the papers. It's a beta trial." It was hard to track the words, though I could hear them all.

"Push the initiators, we need to drop her down." They talked like I wasn't in the room.

Strange alien coldness, vibrating up my arm.

What was going...

Blackness. Whole, deep and complete.

Warmth...

The sea.

Dreams... Dreams like I had always wanted to have. There was the rocky cove, the kelp forest with the good mussels. The strange creatures that sometimes left fish... Tasty fish... Sometimes it was in these round steel things.

Rectangles with bright flashing lights.

Dreams.

So many dreams.

I was an otter. This was not fleeting, no passing flash of distant awareness. This was me. A new life at the closing of an old one. That strange coldness... that vibration.

A new world now... Pushing out towards the waves. Others like me, the chittering, the closeness, the bonding.

New ways to be; to feel, to hope, to know, to love.

Blissful happiness, a completeness never known. A distant life of strange proportions now far from me, like a passing nightmare.

I never wanted it to end.

Forgot it could end.

Forgot everything and learned it all again.

The pull, a vague sensation of up, and expansion- and sunrise. Light building, awareness cracking through the dark. The dream falling away to reality.

No... not again...

Desperately clinging to my last ounce of unconsciousness as if by instinct, awareness rocketed across my perception, wrenching it from me. My eyes snapped open in the tank.

Everything felt different, but not.

My body... somehow... felt like mine.

There was a mask over my muzzle, it bothered me. My forepaws twitched and I drifted in the tank, peering out. Such strange water... Thick viscous fluid...

Memories vaguely flittered in...

I looked down.

My paw... My paw fully formed. I moved it through the thick liquid.

Joy. Everything felt right. This was new... but not...

Wholeness... a completeness I had never known. I had done it. I had found a way to become myself.

A nurse stepped up to the tank; it opened and I was lifted out.

Fluffy towel, and a warm bath... In and out for the next few hours... Heady and drifty... then suddenly, sleep.

Time passed.

"Joyce? Joyce?"

I chittered in curiosity, which melted into a series of happy plaintive barks when I noticed Dr. Andropov. Every part of my body vibrated and wiggled in excitement, as he handed me a voice collar.

Chittering more, I eagerly slid it on.

"Focus, focus, focus, turn on!" It reported. Andropov chuckled.

"I'm an otter! I'm an otter!" spinning around, back arching up instinctively to make up for my long length out of the water, flippers slapping against the bed.

"Easy... Easy... Yes... And quite a lovely otter at that. Welcome back, little vydra, and happy Halloween! You've been asleep a long time. Now I know you're very excited, but I need to run some quick tests," he said.

Same Dr. Andropov, all business.

"Games!" I reported. Same old-new me.

"If you wish. Name?"

"Joyce Coswell." I chirred happily.

"Where are you at the moment?"

"United Earth Medical Center, I think... It smells right."

He made a few notes on his clipboard.

"What are you doing?" I added.

"Just notes, you know the routine," he excused, making more notes.

"But what kind of notes?" He sighed and sat down on the bed next to me, letting me watch.

An explosion of happy chirrs erupted from within.

"You are a most distracting creature," he commented, absently.

"Sorry doc." A low whine punctuated my words.

It was a form, he was making observations. Strangely it was marked "classified". Oh, he probably shouldn't have been showing me that. It was a secret.

Extreme curiosity, reduced attention, play-oriented. Animalistic vocalizations, degree of integration 95.2 %- Patient stable in spite of threshold violation.

I felt special.

"Hyperactive as always, and a bit distractible." He snapped his finger, then waved his clipboard; my neck vertebrae popped from my sudden movement trying to track it all.

"But everything seems to be in order. From everything I can see here, you are a normal and healthy Sea Otter, if a bit more erudite," he smiled. "Now, are you feeling up for visitors?" he asked.

"Yes please!" I responded eagerly, sitting up in the bed on my hind flippers, forepaws hanging in front, eagerly watching the door.

He patted my head and walked out.

"Hey there Aqua Girl, happy Halloween, love the costume," John said, entering.

Like an otter sized missile, I rocketed across the room, and pushed up against him emitting a happy chirr.

"Hey there, whoa, I missed you too."

"You've lost weight, I'm hungry, do you want to eat? It's great to see you!" The excitement was driving my hyperactivity. My elation burning like an undying fire. *I was an otter*

"Do you want me to answer those in list or essay form?" he chuckled, and gently patted the fur on the top of my head.

In an act of instinct, I pushed up into it, twitching my forepaw with a happy chitter.

"Look at me! Look at me!" I spun around, full of vanity.

A deep look of longing crossed his face and it immediately grounded me some, and I snuggled back up to him, in an effort to comfort.

"Your day will come, and I'll be there. Just like you were for me. I promise. Trust me, its greater than you will ever imagine," I assured.

My life renewed, I was born again.

Chapter 18

It's funny what you have to get used to when you change your species.

I was learning to live with having to wear a harness.

During my time in the tank, the UEA had passed the Morphic Sentience Act, updating a series of old laws, and bringing them into congruence with the changing world. This ensured I had no fear of things like Animal Control officers ruining my day.

However, it also mandated that ferals wear a harness or vest, with "Human Equivalent Intelligence" clearly visible from either side to tell us apart from our feral cousins. It was somewhat understandable, but also annoying; it required a collar, but I was still capable of speech.

I felt like a service otter.

Kelowna, B.C. was icy cold, but my insulated fur provided ample barrier, not to mention the black harness covering my torso, proclaiming my sentience for all to see.

"Keep up fish breath, I'm sorry I have to do this so quick," John said, walking as quickly as his dignity allowed.

"I know you have orders, I'm just grateful you are putting me up," I replied. Ricky was still in the tank until the end of November. In the chaotic moments surrounding my tanking, this one detail had slipped through the cracks.

There was no place for me to stay until the ship launched in December.

And so, the cabin, though not ideal, was better than living with my feral cousins off Monterey Bay.

John entered the small supermarket; I followed in after him and the place stopped, turned and looked at me.

One woman screamed something about a wild animal, another person asked if they should notify the police.

A nervous looking, and overworked store manager ran up to John. "Sir, You're going to need to leave your pet outside."

"I'm not his pet. I'm his friend, and I'd like to buy some tuna cans," I snapped, through my collar.

"Oh... Um... Yes... you're one of them. I'm sorry. Um... Can you wait...." He began to say the words but John cut him off.

"She's wearing her harness, so she's publicly decent. She's got her ID tags, and her HEI designators. Leave her alone," John ordered, cutting an imposing figure in his fatigues.

"Oh yes... the Act... I got a memo. Everyone, everyone, It's ok, I assure you there is no sanitation issue," he announced.

I was mortified.

In that moment, Centioc One could not come fast enough.

The manager nodded as if admitting defeat.

"Please, just be quick," he pleaded.

Angry barks followed, along with a stomping protest just because I was angry.

The quick trip became torturous, as all eyes followed us as we roamed the supermarket. People whispered, pointed and stared.

Some took pictures, but no one asked.

"Joyce, you don't have to stay. I wouldn't blame you for going back to the car," John urged, all worries of his orders, at the moment, gone.

"No, I'm not leaving. I don't have the problem. **They have a problem**," I said loudly through my voice collar.

He smiled. "Fuck em."

"Fuck em," I confirmed, just as loudly, bouncing around in a loop.

We decided to take our time, strolled, considered a few things.

The sun was down by the time we got to John's cabin; it was out in the middle of nowhere, ten minutes down a dirt road.

A green light in the yard briefly distracted me as I watched John unload the bags.

"That's where the deliveries get dropped," he mentioned, passing by with the last two bags in tow from the rental car.

Scurrying up the stairs and entering the cabin, I explored around the small space. It was old and smelled of deep aged woods. There was a faint scent, like John's, but different, especially in the second bedroom, that had been converted into a study.

There were door handles, not knobs, all of them new; something the workers must have replaced when John had them in earlier. I was just tall enough, I could reach them and manipulate them with a paw.

"So what do you think, do ya approve?" He checked his watch again.

"It's fine, I'll manage," I urged, knowing he had to go.

"Ok. I'm so sorry this has to be so quick." He patted my head fur again.

"It's been four days, I don't know how you managed. Just don't get yourself thrown in the brig," I demanded.

He chuckled. "I'll be fine, but yeah, I'll check in when I can." He knelt down and I pressed close to him in my best approximation of a hug.

"Thank you John, for everything," I chirred. "I wish you didn't have to go," I continued.

"I know, but it will only be a couple of weeks," he replied.

Heavy boots moved across the floor and the vibrations tickled the edges of my hind flippers as John walked out.

Silence descended upon the cabin like a snowy shroud.

I had been out of the tank for four days, three in observation at United Earth and now here. My world, with its constant movement, with every single day focused on on one goal, came to a screeching halt.

The revelation rocketed over me. This was it, what I had suffered and hoped for. It was my first night to myself, *as an otter*.

My mind raced with possibilities, as I began to become aware of and distracted by the tiny noises that inhabited the old cabin like ghosts.

Bath, Tuna, Cartoons.

Chirrr... That sounded nice.

Wait, why not take it further?

Bath *with* tuna and cartoons...

A series of barks and excited chirps escaped my throat as the possibilities of that idea bloomed to full brilliance.

Hurray for waterproof tablets.

The bathroom had a lever faucet, and a tub with a shower head.

Flexing my forepaws, I was able to work it without much trouble. Much of the stiffness and restriction reduced, now that I was away from the shift.

While the tub filled with hot water, I quickly moved down the hall, gathered up a few cans in a bag and dragged them along with me.

I elected to carry the screwdriver in my muzzle.

Making it barely in time, I cut off the hot water with a slap to the lever, and let some of the water drain; setting my tablet on the edge, I slid in, and then righted myself, my body knowing what to do.

A torrent of happy chitter came with a wave of deep relaxation as the heat and the water took the strain off my muscles and skeleton.

My thoughts drifted back to tuna and cartoons. With a few more feats of acrobatics, and getting water everywhere, I soon had an empty can of tuna on a plastic plate on my chest. Lazily, I ate while my tablet played my favorites.

Some light grooming ensued... and then... sleep.

Drifting... floating in the water; it cooled, but the air trapped within my fur kept me warm.

Blissful, happy day.

I could truly get used to this.

Chapter 19

"On old Olympus' towering tops, A fine Victorian gentlemen viewed a hawk," I repeated to myself, bouncing and dancing on paws and flippers as I recited the words. A mnemonic device, learned in college to remember the twelve human cranial nerves.

License re-certification. The UEA wanted to make sure I still knew how to be a nurse.

Just another hurdle before embarkment on December 15th.

It was the end of November, and my time at the cabin, was wearing at its edge. It was quiet. There was no place to swim, no one to talk to. Desperate for stimulation, I had resorted to doing paperwork.

It had gotten that bad.

Taking off into a jog around the house, bouncing and bounding, my hindquarters slid out to the left or right as I lost traction on the laminate flooring. Movement cleared my head, and helped me to focus.

Sitting still had become a torment.

The ever present momentum of a lifetime of wanting, followed by the rush of fulfilling, had crashed upon the shores of the sleepy cabin, deep in the BC forest, and rolled back, leaving an uneasy peace amid the quiet of my temporary home.

Chitters and barks disrupted the meditative atmosphere as I finished my run and decided to chase my tail a bit. Why not, what else was there to do?

Setting my paws on an open book on the table, I sighed and got back to reading. Allowing the cartoons to play on the screen provided regular, and needed distraction.

Watch me juggle, watch me dance.

A building sense of frustration ate at me, as I let my head thud heavily onto the anatomy book open on the coffee table.

I still knew all these nursing things.

Bored.

Maybe another practice test? That had been fun.

Yeah the first ten times.

Ugh!

"Lonely," I said to myself, through the collar. There was only my canary to keep me company, and I had seen the one playing out currently on the screen many times before.

I thought about John. We were in a radio silence period while he finished up aboard the Danube. Bi-weekly messages had been coming in regularly. It was a lifeline that had buoyed my sanity as the weeks stretched longer and colder out in the woods.

Slapping my paw down on the tablet, it chimed.

"Sol News Network- Stream FX," I ordered, a confirmation tone soon followed and the stream began to play.

Bored with my textbook, I devolved into a few moments of dancing, as a man in a cowboy hat tried to sell me on a class action lawsuit as he made his pitch for financial glory between the newscasts.

-

"Call the law offices of Canwe, Cheatem and Hou," I said distantly through the collar in my best announcer voice.

"More threats of violence against Shift Clinics set to open next week, as the Beta Program draws to a close. The first morphics now beginning to appear in society as the world holds its breath. An official statement released by the UEA Diplomatic Corps hailed the close of the program as the beginning of a new golden era for our world, with the help of our Mendian allies.

Ricky and Sonya would be getting out of the tank in a few days, and next week, we would see each other for the first time, as ourselves.

Deep excitement pulled at me, as the eight days before that event stretched out like a frozen road in winter.

It seemed so far away.

Officially, it was training, Zero G certification and safety workshops, but it was also reunion day.

It was going to be a pool party.

The idea of swimming, seeing my friends and lots of good food and play made my paws tingle with eagerness, as a few impatient barks punctuated my thoughts.

It couldn't come fast enough.

"In other news, the CEO of Martian Maraurder Logistics announced plans for new trade routes to the future Colony on Centioc One. As our viewers are familiar, the shipping magnate's son is currently undergoing shifting, and is among the first 250 in the Beta Program.

Mack, they were talking about Mack. All of my focus grew fixated on the newscast.

"Buoyed by this news, stocks surged higher, sparking early rumors of a colonial boom, if the Centioc Colony Project proves successful.

It felt strange to be a part of history. They were talking about my friends and I, things we were planning to do, and had already done.

The boredom drained away as excitement seized me. Pioneers on the new frontier.

My tablet rang, and my heart leaped up into my throat, inspiring a series of vocalizations, dominated by a whining low chirping moan.

Mom was calling.

Had she seen the report? I froze. It had been over a year since we had talked. There had been a fiery falling out over my decision to tank.

They said they had needed time after that, and I was only too happy to give it to them.

Defiance boiled up in me along with pride, as I answered with video, syncing my tablet with the Screen in the living room.

Only her picture avatar showed, but a small picture in the picture window at the lower left corner showed I was broadcasting.

"Joyce? Is that you?" Her tone sounded anguished, worried.

"Yeah Mom. Hi." The words were clumsy; it was all unrehearsed, how else do you break the news?

"Jerry, Jerry, come to the screen, see what your daughter has done to herself," she called out distantly, back into her condo. Her tone intending to shame me.

It was the game she had played her entire life, and I resented her for it. Passive aggressive tones and quips ensued, distant hinting acknowledgment of her disapproval of my life and my choices.

This was the wedge she could never comprehend, that had always driven us apart.

She wanted me to live my life her way. She wanted me to be the person she saw me as, not what I was, not who I aspired to be.

In her mind, I had always been her little girl to shape, but that wasn't my truth.

I was no human girl, and never had been, regardless of my human days.

Not even my formerly primate brain could take the otter I was- out of my soul.

The fetid environment of old unhealed battles blossomed into a new and septic wound.

"Step right up, don't be shy. Freak on display," I spat bitterly.

"Now honey, don't be like that. Just because we don't agree with your choices, a little tolerance on your end would be welcome," she chided. Taking the high ground.

"Oh. I'm sorry, I thought you were selling tickets when I heard how you called Dad," I replied bitterly.

"Don't lay into your mother like that Doodlebug. We haven't heard from you in well over a year, and then you go off and do this tanking nonsense." More subtle swipes. Aggressive jabs, couched in civility.

Angry chitters erupted from my throat. "It's not nonsense, and it never was. You've just never listened. My whole life. I tried to tell you, tried to show you how bad I was hurting but you never saw it. You just kept pushing. Always pushing. Be this, do that, think this way. You can't..." Growling, I lost my thought briefly before continuing...

"I wasn't a computer for you to program god dammit, I'm your daughter. I have a will and this is me. It always has been. You just ignored it," my forepaws tingled. An angry modulating growl punctuated my words as I bared my teeth, elements of my animal nature shining through.

"Honey you sound like a wild animal..." Desperation now, no finely crafted assaults, at least it was real... Progress.

"I am. It's who I've always been. You just don't see. Remember how you told me it was a phase. That there was a time I had to start growing up, stop playing pretend and put my childish games away? No matter how hard I tried, it always felt like suicide. Someone had to go, me or the lie, so I decided to start being me." The words fell, like stones impacting on heavy pavement.

The sound of tears spilled from the other end of the line. Shame pelted me, wrapped around my heart like a warm acid and crackled within my chest. Ugliness and bile.

Part of me wanted to vomit. Disgusted, angry, fed up and suddenly tired.

"We're just never going to agree on your choices or who you are I'm afraid," my Dad reported over the line.

"You're going to have to tolerate them at least if you want to be in my life. They've become too much of who I am to ignore." A chitter escaped as if to add specific punctuation to the point.

"Alright sweetheart. Well. We're glad you're happy. We love you," Dad replied, more sounds of distant crying coming from Mom.

I cut the vid feed, dropping to audio.

"Yeah. Sure. Love ya too," I replied, bitterly.

The line went dead.

Suddenly I felt every reason to focus on my studies.

Chapter 20

A simple rental shuttle was landing in the yard. I was in my harness, eager to get underway to Boston for my re-certification test.

The ramp lowered and a small banded tail kangaroo rat, almost a feral, but not quite, bounded down with fidgety movements.

"Yo freak, ya ride is here," Kevin intoned, with his textbook acerbity.

Skittering forward, barely able to contain my excitement, it had been a week since I had talked to anyone.

I fear I may have worn grooves into the floor of the cabin for all the laps I had made, bounding on flippers and paws.

"Have you looked in the mirror lately, guinea pig?" I challenged, our normal game.

He bounded up in a set of frenetic movements and hugged.

"Hey what do I know, I'm just a rat and a chauffeur," he shrugged, gesticulating with his tiny front paws that he kept dangling in front of him, always at the ready, always moving.

That, combined with his sarcastic nature made him unintentionally adorable.

"If ya ready, we should get underway to Logan Spaceport, wife is expecting us for lunch," Kevin continued. My stomach rumbled.

Home cooked anything after a month on cans sounded amazing.

In truth, since my shift, any food sounded amazing. My hunger was near constant, my metabolism much higher.

"Oh, of course, and thank you for going to the trouble," I replied, remembering my manners, fidgeting myself.

We made quite the pair.

"Eh, don't mention it. I've been wicked bored since I got out the tank. Munchkin is with the grandparents while we pack up the condo. Needed to get away, it was nothin," he replied.

Fumbling with the chest harness, I managed to get myself belted in. Kevin's new posture had him almost hovering over the seat, his natural configuration, now similar in angle to a humans sitting position.

"So how ya liking being you?" he asked, as the clearances came in and we began to alight to the atmosphere.

"I'm loving it, but I've been so bored, nothing to do but paperwork, study or cartoons. The news is too depressing."

"Ya it's something else isn't it? I've got this wicked long tail to contend with, but hey, it's actually kinda fun, but you're right about the news. Glad to be leaving," he shrugged, tapping the controls a few more times, making adjustments.

"When's your family gonna join you out there?" I asked. He was the only one on the committee with a full family. I couldn't imagine the sacrifices they were making.

"Condo goes on the market in January; they hope to set out by next July. Let Gwen finish out her second grade year, get things settled and give us time to get something built out there," he replied.

We hit the top of the arch and began to descend towards Boston; transcontinentals were short, half an hour, tops.

"Long time be apart," I replied.

"Don't I know it. Been doing this for years, Joyce. Go out for six months on the ort runs, then back home for shore leave, maintenance and then another six months out. Tired of just watching her grow up only half the time. Tired of missing birthdays. This way, we can afford to get out of the city, a little land and I got to shift. Come January, we spend our last six months apart. Our last goodbye. Afterwards I get to be a father full time." He was rambling, I had never seen him so sincere. He stared off out from the cockpit windows, full of hope.

"You never told me you were a softie," I teased, and he squeaked at me in angry tones.

"Hey now. That's how ya go treating a guy that opens up. The nerve of you west coast hippies," he scolded.

A playful cacophony of chitters abounded as a giggle escaped through my voice collar.

"Oh yeah, laugh it up chuckles. I need a ride Kevin, pick up the shuttle Kevin, fly me to Centioc Kevin. I know when I'm being used." He played up the hurt, even drooping his tiny ears.

"Regular sad sack. Should I get the violin?" I challenged.

He playfully reached out with his small right hand paw and shoved me, which elicited an angry chitter in response.

"Whoa there killer, remember you need me to land this tub," he replied.

Rain was falling on the shuttle as it glided into its covered port at landing pad D.

The ramp lowered and we followed the signs along the moving walkway into the Logan International Space Port.

Another leftover from the age of air travel; it was a morass of renovations, and dreams crashed into bureaucracy, graft and overreach. In a way, its levels and contrasting designs were historical. Illustrating certain scandals or hopes that collided against the inevitable bottom lines and budgets of reality.

"Come on Joyce, we gotta make our train, or we are stuck here for another hour," Kevin urged.

I pulled in my body, increasing my arch and bounced faster on paws and flippers as he increased his bounding stride. Dimly, I became aware of people watching the spectacle of us move, but my focus remained on the long bobbing tail of my kangaroo rat friend. Not only did it feel like a game of chase, I had no idea how well I'd navigate this place alone.

After almost a month in a cabin in BC, the space port alone felt overwhelming, like being thrown into the deep end of a pool.

Finally the platform; more whispers, points and stares. Kevin and I were among the first few hundred morphics in the world and quite a novelty. A ring of interested people soon surrounded us, and Kevin took out a vest from a small backpack he was carrying.

It was maroon in color and built for his form, but on the back in large letters, it read "DO NOT PET." He turned and winked at me.

An angry squealing noise rose suddenly from his throat and the crowd stepped back another three feet, attempting to act as if they were ignoring us.

Finally, our train came, and I was grateful to be aboard it.

Still, it only changed the type of fishbowl I had found myself in.

Thirty more minutes of whispers, stares and bible tracts followed.

"Almost there Joyce," Kevin assured me.

"Is it always like this? Geeze, it's nerve-racking." A woman overhearing our conversation, turned and made her way to an open seat, and sat down with a dejected look on her face.

At this point, it felt like I should have sold tickets.

"Can be, depends on the day. We're the newest freaks of the week and humans gotta gawk," he shrugged.

"Fuck em," he continued. "They can have this fried dirt ball of a planet, I got my own."

It occurred to me he was absolutely right.

Chapter 21

I could smell the water of Quincy Bay. The University of Massachusetts was situated right on its edge, and I longed to dive in the frigid water, swim and be free, *but today wasn't meant for that*, I reminded myself. The whole reason I had come here, now loomed before me like an imposing mountain; after two days with Kevin and his wife, Maria, it had all come down to this.

Re-certification day; if this went wrong, if I failed, the colony would be short a medic.

Would that mean I'd be stuck here, on Earth, with no options?

The thought terrified me, I hadn't considered that before.

"Miss Coswell? Right this way." A woman wearing a sharp business suit looked up from her clipboard, gesturing to me to follow along. I leapt up in nervousness.

"Sure. Um thanks. What's first?" I asked, my tone showing my nervousness through my voice collar.

"General knowledge test first, your basic license re-certification you're accustomed to every two years or so, but after that, we have a special test to make sure you can actually function in the role. If so, you'll be the first in your field." Her tone was informative, detached, yet casual as she led me to a room filled with desks with tablet screens inlaid into them.

"Alright let's begin. Find a seat that suits you and I'll load the first tests in. You'll have forty-five minutes for each section. Failure to complete, is an automatic failure. Do you understand?" she continued.

I swallowed, hard; a concerned chirp escaped my throat, to which she raised an eyebrow. Two other individuals, one male and one female, both in business attire entered, taking a seat at the front of the classroom.

"Yes, I think I do," I replied, and with trembling paws, took a seat at the center.

"Ready to begin?" she asked, tapping at her clipboard tablet again; the screen inlaid into the desk activated.

"Yes," I reported, my responses quipped by the situation I found myself in.

"In accordance with the Morphic Sentience Act, we've made every effort to make the test accessible. Begin," she reported. A timer appeared in the upper right hand corner of my screen, as she took the center seat between the two other monitors.

forty-four Minutes, fifty-nine seconds remaining.

The morning devolved into a near endless series of questions, trick and otherwise. The terror of what might happen if I messed up kept me hyper-focused, as I tore into the tests mercilessly.

I had been a nurse for two years, and been doing nothing but studying for the last month; they proved no challenge.

I passed with a 99.5%.

The monitor that had given me the test looked slightly annoyed. "Well, that was unexpected," she reported, as her eyes narrowed at the tablet displaying my real time results.

"Excuse me?" I asked, my nervousness suddenly parted like clouds, revealing a rising angry sun just behind it.

She straightened up, as if remembering I could hear her and understand what she was saying. "Nothing. This way." Her tone was clipped, and her body language was rigid.

I don't think she liked me.

She gestured to the man that had been monitoring my exam for the last three hours.

"This is Dr. MacGuiness. He will be running you through the real life tests, and conducting your medical and psychiatric evaluation. Good day." She turned and left, without ever giving her name.

I watched as she left, her form still rigid; heels clicking on the hard tile floor.

"Ma'am?" I heard the doctor, but I was distracted.

"Miss Coswell?" He asked again. I turned my head towards him, blinking in a kind of stupor.

"I'm sorry, it's been a full day," I excused.

"That's perfectly alright. Sarah can have that effect on people. Cold as nor'easter; don't let her demeanor worry you, she's a bitch to everyone," he explained, and I fell to giggles.

"I thought it might be the way I am," I suggested, referencing my form.

"Oh I have no doubt that's the heart of it, but she doesn't like anybody. Don't let it throw you. As for me, I volunteered to assess you," he admitted. His blue eyes sparkled, and blazed in contrast to his white lab coat and silver grey hair. He was handsome, for a human.

"Why's that?" I coaxed, seeking more information.

"You'll be the first morphic with a medical certification. Kind of historic, if you pass muster. Considering your test scores, I don't see that being a huge problem. Beyond all that though, I just wanted to meet you. It's a fascinating idea really, and I hope you don't mind questions," he explained.

"As long as you aren't a jerk about it, I'll answer whatever you want to know." His easy demeanor relaxed me.

"Well, follow me and we'll get your examination out of the way, and we can talk some," he offered, gesturing down the hallway.

"Sounds good," I replied.

Another two hours of being poked and prodded passed by while the doctor grilled me on the whole gambit; from tanking, to the boosters, I shared it all. While he ran me through function tests, neurological assessments, the works, I followed him from room, to room to room; as the day wore on, in each room lay another challenge.

By the time the clock was showing 4 PM, I was both exhausted and starving. It had been a long day.

"Fascinating," he replied. As I told him about the dreams I had while in the tank. I was holding a simulated arm, of a simulated patient, attempting to place an auto dropper, which was an assistive device for nurses with limited dexterity, and for students still learning. It set up IVs, so I didn't have to hold a needle.

Clever technology, if only I could get my paws to cooperate with it. He eyed me worriedly, as I struggled with the device.

"Having trouble?" he asked, and I suddenly felt the tension return.

"No, I'll get it; my paws sometimes don't like to cooperate. I've always been a little clumsy," I excused, and he made a note on his tablet that he carried.

Shit. It fueled my desperation, which made me fumble, but finally, on my fourth attempt, I successfully dropped a line on the dummy.

Joy and elation swept through me, as I sagged down.

"See, told ya I'd get it," I reported with pride.

"Yes. You've done very well today. I don't see any reason why you shouldn't be re-certified," he reported.

My heart leapt, I was about to make history, again.

"I'll make my recommendations, and submit the forms. Do you mind waiting about an hour more?" he asked.

"No, not at all. Back up front right? Would it be ok to head out on campus? I'd love to find a food court," I replied.

"I don't see why not, I really appreciate you answering all my personal questions. I'd love to have you talk to a few of my classes, maybe get some of your fellow morphics along, but I know you're leaving in a few weeks." He tapped at his screen a few times.

"Yeah, but not forever. I don't plan on just staying; I'm sure I'll come back to visit. Let's stay in touch, and see what happens." He smiled at that, and offered his hand.

"Miss Coswell, it's been a pleasure." I reached out with my left forepaw, and grasped as best I could, in a modified shake; he squeezed, then released and left.

Chapter 22

I had caused a small stir in the commons ordering three burgers and, thus, had made certain my order was to-go. Upon receiving the grease stained white bag, I carried it in my muzzle, as I beat a path back across the campus towards the Integrated Sciences Building. Once there, I made camp in a chair in the corner, while I eagerly awaited the final results of my re-certification.

It was nearing 1700 hours; the last classes of the afternoon were letting out, and my eating was drawing a crowd.

Everything I did seemed to draw a crowd; as Kevin had said, we were the freaks of the week.

It was hard to get accustomed to, the living in a fish bowl. I wondered idly, if this is how a celebrity felt. Everywhere I went in public, people either reacted with fear, curiosity or a mix in between, but few took the time to treat me as a person, like Dr. MacGuiness had. Most just went for the novelty angle.

"Aww, she's holding the patty in her paws like a little person," a female undergraduate remarked, clutching her books tightly to her chest.

"I am a person, and you're being an asshole," I said through my collar, not bothering to stop eating. It was one of its many advantages.

"You don't have to be so rude about it," she snapped back.

"Yeah, and you don't have to treat me like a carnival show, but we all make our choices." I growled a bit, defiantly. I was tired, and sick of this. The cabin in Kelowna had been so quiet, I was desperate to get back out into the world. Now, all I wanted was to run back to it.

"Bitch." She threw one last insult before turning to storm out in a huff. *Way to go Joyce, making friends everywhere.*

Just a little while longer before Kevin arrived, I got my results and then it was back to the obscurity of the woods; I was exhausted from being stared at.

I finished my burger and decided to address the gawking crowd.

"Does anyone have any questions that don't revolve around my eternal soul, or how adorable I am?" I asked, my voice tipped with annoyance.

People looked at each other nervously, some wrung their hands.

"I'm a person, a fuzzy person, but I'm a person just like you. I know it's new, I know it's unusual, but I'm nothing to be afraid of, I just want to go about my business like any other normal individual," I continued.

"But you aren't normal. You're a freak." It was Sarah, the monitor from before; she had pushed through the small crowd that was now disbursing.

"And you're a real bitch. I know someone who can help you be the real you. His name is Dr. Andropov." I had, had it.

She narrowed her eyes at me, and tapped a few keys on her tablet.

"You're re-certified, now get the fuck out of here before I call security," she threatened.

"Or what? This is a public university, and I have business here. Maybe I'll go to the library, and read. What are you going to do about it?" I swear her eyes flashed red with fury. She went to open her mouth, and then turned and left.

Kevin appeared, bounding through the door, and I don't know if I've ever been so grateful to see someone.

"Oh thank God," I said audibly, as Sarah stormed off in a huff.

"How'd it go, hippie?" he asked.

"It's not been so bad, except being on display, how do you get used to this?" I asked.

"Oh, well, you just have to learn my mantra, repeat after me, Fuck em and feed em fish heads," he intoned, and I forgot my anger, laughing out loud through my collar.

"Fish heads?" I asked. As he gestured to me, I began to follow him out towards the shuttle; we were on our way home.

"See, it works, got your mind off it didn't it?" he replied.

Chapter 23

The sound of keys sliding into the lock and turning greeted me. It was a needless action, I didn't keep the doors in the cabin locked. In truth, I saw little need to out here.

It had been two days since Boston, and my world had again descended into a quiet waiting.

I rocketed up from the couch, and centered myself in front of the door expectantly. There was only one person who it could be.

John appeared as the door opened, and I chittered happily, rocketing towards him.

"Hey there Aqua Girl, it's good to see you, too," he said, drawing me into a hug. I felt his head turn as he looked around.

"God Joyce, there are empty tuna cans stacked everywhere," he said, surveying the damage.

The cabin had taken on a slightly lived-in look.

Plaintive chirps preceded my words. "I'm sorry. It's what I like to eat, and the trash pickup only comes every two weeks.

That alone had been a challenge. I was about four feet, six inches in length, so I had some size to me, but dragging the bag along while I maneuvered on three paws proved challenging.

"And why are you using lawn bags?" he asked, trying to puzzle out the mysteries of my solitary existence these last few weeks.

"Hard to carry things, and balance on my flippers, easier to limp along on three, so I drag stuff… was making a terrible mess in the yard, though it was fun to chase the plates," I admitted.

"Clever. You're adapting well," he complimented.

"I've kind of had to, but it's not hard. The fact that I know how to use my body makes it a lot easier. You can't look at it like a disability, it's not. It's not a loss of function, it's a difference in function, requires a rethink." There were a lot of things I couldn't do as an otter that I could do as a human, but there were also many things I could now do as an otter that humans will never aspire to.

The skill set dovetailed with my identity; the tradeoff seemed more than equitable.

"Seeing you makes it easier for me," John replied.

That old thing.

"You're still having that debate? Be a hare. Don't be silly," I chided, and I saw him blush.

"You know I've always been on the fence. Quadruped seems amazing, but I do so much with computers, and work on ships. How do I make the two fit?" His eyes took on a far, pained look.

"I'm still a nurse, re-certified and everything. There are things I can't do, instruments I can't hold right, but that's not a barrier to me providing care, expertise, empathy. You're a math geek, you can teach, you can talk. Also, I still have thumbs. They don't have the flexibility or the range of motion, but watch this." I reached out and grasped the screwdriver, with little effort.

"Practice makes perfect." I said with pride.

"Even can kind of ham fist hold a pen if I take the time to work it between the paw pads now. It's crude and kinda hurts, but I was able to sign my name like I was five again, and was really proud to do so when I finished the test for my re-certification. The longer I live with its challenges, the more I learn to beat them. Don't let the fears of function hold you back," I urged.

"So that means it won't be any problem for you to help me clean this place," he pivoted, and pinned me with his point.

An angry bark of defiance. "That was a dirty trick John Dawkins."

He opened a lawn bag. "Get cracking, Aqua Girl."

It was nice not to have to drag the bags. That was annoying.

After an hour of work, the cabin was restored. There were two new bags of recycling, out in the pick-up crates.

"Hungry," I reported, and darted over towards my stack of cans.

"I think salmon, for a snack... Maybe a tuna chaser," I mused, idly.

"That's what? Three cans since lunch. Hungry much?" He chided.

"I have a metabolism that rivals a fusion reactor. Always, always *hungry*." Driven by need and eagerness, I tore into the can with the screwdriver, wrenching off its lid. With practiced motiones, I smacked it down on the wax paper plate in just the right way. There was a plop noise, and a perfect mound of pink fish appeared as I raised the can slowly with both paws up off the dish.

"That explains all the ring imprints I'm finding around," he observed.

"Hey, a girl has to eat," I replied and shrugged.

He got up and walked to the kitchen, then a series of cabinets opened and shut.

"Not much here for me, but I could use a bite. Think I'll get a pizza, maybe burgers."

My stomach growled. "Burgers?"

"You just ate," he reminded.

"That was then, this is now." It had been a busy day anyway.

"Ok, ok. You want to ride along... Joyce?"

I had already disappeared into the bedroom and was on my way back with my harness before he finished calling my name.

"Yes please."

He helped me slip it on, saving me at least a half hour of fumbling with its magnetic clasp. It was supposedly designed with my forepaws in mind.

At least they tried.

"Pool party tomorrow, you're still coming right?" I asked, as we loaded into the car and began the quest.

The forest quickly swallowed us; it was just after 5 PM and already dark.

"Of course, actually kind of looking forward to it. It's been an insane amount of work this last year. They've been running us ragged to get this tech out and tested," John complained.

"You have lost weight you know. Really, you look like you've been working hard," I commented, watching the dark world whizz by around me, only occasionally illumined by a light in the distance, or the glow from the windows of a passing house.

The blinking lights of shuttles, high overhead in alternating blinking bands provided counterpoint to our terrestrial movement, as people came and went across the planet.

"If I never see, eat or taste another ration bar ever again, I'll be the happiest person on this or any planet," John said.

"Ration bars?" I asked; the Danube was a functional ship, they weren't out in the field.

"Retrofit had a lot of her systems offline, and they are "Nutritionally complete, calorically balanced and optimized for peak nutrition," he shrugged.

"One thing you learn after being in a few years, is that there's the normal way that life works, and then there's the way Central Command works. There's no understanding it from outside, and there's no understanding it from inside. Their decisions are forces of nature. You can curse the wind, but you can't fight it. It is what it is," John shared his hard won wisdom.

"So, in this case, that meant ration bars," I repeated, trying to make sure I had the point.

"Yep, ration bars. Probably because they had a surplus of em or something. They don't tell you why; they just expect you to report and function until you don't."

"Yet you still signed up, in for the full seven," I countered. The forest began to break. Kelowna began to become visible ahead, its night lights shining brightly, as if in competition with the sky.

"Got me out of B.C., and into space, so yeah, I signed up, would do it again. Met a certain Aqua Girl at JFA because of that seven contract," He reached over with one hand, keeping an eye on the road, and playfully shoved me.

I barked in reply.

"Fair. It's like I was saying earlier. You already know. You take the good with the bad, you learn and adapt." The conversation had come full circle.

A hushed quiet found the car and seemed to capture the both of us, as the lights in the cabin brightened as we came under the street lights of the sleepy minor city hidden in the woods.

Just after 630 now, and already shutting down for the night.

"You want to go in or drive thru?" he asked, as we entered the shopping area of the town.

"Drive thru, not in the mood to be on display, been too nice of a day for a fight," I replied, picking my battles.

"Fair," he replied.

Chapter 24

"Party, party, party." I danced in a tight loop, as John emerged down the ramp of the shuttle in bathing trunks and a fun run shirt. He pulled his jacket around him tightly, not in any way dressed for San Jose in January.

It felt strange being back here after all this time.

"I know, I know," he admitted good naturedly.

"Sorry." One of the interesting challenges about being the newer, better 'me' was there was no off switch for my enthusiasm.

My long exile had finally ended. Happy memories of last night, falling asleep next to John on the couch after two burger patties down and a can of tuna, coupled with the excitement that today, I would be swimming- had me in a relaxed, but hyper state.

We had watched a classic horror movie, "Creature From The Black Lagoon". He said it jived with the current aquatic theme in our life.

I think he was being a smart ass.

In two other places around the world, this process was repeating, a two-day celebration. The first day, a 'getting to know you' pool party, and the second Zero G training, and ship safety briefings, in the very same pools.

The Beta Program was closed; everyone was out of the tank and now, we had fourteen days left until we got underway to Centioc One.

It was time for last things.

Moving along quickly on the concrete path. We soon came to a large arena-like entrance.

Slipping in was like stepping into a new world.

About forty morphics of various mammalian species, sizes and configurations were all milling about the room, socializing and chatting with interspersed humans, mainly friends and family, along with some staff.

"Hey there sweetheart. No more wheel chair," Ricky smiled, he looked a humanoid ocelot. About 5'4, with a long tail; retractable claws marked the end of his hand paws and hind paws.

Sonya was a much more blended red panda, but far from being as feral as me. She was still bipedal for one. Her paws were also much more humanoid and had greater dexterity; the thumb was fully present and uninhibited. Her bushy, raccoon like tail, with its red and white coloration, swayed gently, drawing my attention. Two triangular ears dotted the top of her head, with fuzzy fur puffed-up around it.

"You look so fluffy dry," she commented, and I chirped at the praise.

"Don't expect it to stay that way today, but I groom, a lot... It calms me," I admitted.

"Join the club," Sonya mentioned as I caught Ricky flick his ear in cat-like fashion.

No more monsters ball, or Kronenberg days. My friends, as themselves.

"Hey there, Hey there!" Kevin bounced up, with a young girl, about seven years old chasing after him, attached to his now incredibly long banded tail, easily the length of his own body.

"Hey there guinea pig," I greeted him.

"Yo, sea loving freak," he answered, his hand like fore paws hung in front of him. He was about 4'8, just barely taller than me, but his arched frame made him appear smaller.

"Daddy, I want to swim," the little girl complained, and tugged on his tail.

A series of squeaks escaped his small pointed muzzle, as his whiskers twitched.

"Gwen, sweetheart, don't tug, that hurts," he corrected. She looked down sullenly.

"It's ok Princess, let's go find mommy and get in the water," he offered. She perked up, immediately appeased.

"Later, alright?" he bounced; everything about him seemed more frenetic, but his playful, acerbic nature still shone through.

None of us had changed in the exact same way. There was no method to the madness that predicted precisely how our personalities changed with our forms. It was a personal, and unique calculus that played out in ways that consistently surprised me.

"Swim sounds nice," I announced, eager for the water, fumbling with the straps of my harness.

I looked over to John and he knelt down and began to help me with it.

"I see that I've gotten you trained," I remarked, sarcastically.

"You been doing ok, man?" Ricky asked.

"Oh yeah," John replied, helping me get the final strap loose, as the last ones slipped free.

It reminded me of wearing a bra; the best part of wearing them was taking them off.

"They've been keeping us real busy. Running us through drills. Working with the new tech." He unceremoniously grabbed me, heaved me up and threw me in the water.

Diving in, knowing instinctively what to do, I righted myself, and my long body straightened out, flippers and tail kicked in and I was underway, gliding through the water back up the side, soon hanging my forepaws over the edge of the pool singing in angry chitter.

"John Dawkins, you asshole!" I shouted through my collar. Though waterproof, the speaker became muffled wet, making me nigh unintelligible.

A series of howling fits of animalistic laughter erupted from my group, with John leading the charge.

"Oh, been waiting forever to do that," he confessed, which earned another tirade of angry barks from me.

Ricky and John devolved into a brief moment of horseplay before Sonya shoved them in, tumbling in after them.

"Hey, you four, chill out," a lifeguard angrily scolded us.

"Sorry." We all quickly excused ourselves.

I dove down and made a few quick laps before reemerging. My first real chance to swim since exiting the tank. Not a bath, but a massive pool.

On land, I was awkward, my body bunched up and I kind of bounced when I moved, because though amphibious, I was truly built for water.

In water, everything straightened out, everything felt perfectly supported and it was like I could *fly*. Darting through the water like a tiny, reddish brown missile.

A dive, a flip, a quick lap around the pool again and again.

Cresting, rolling and drifting on my back, I floated by John, lazily.

"Hi there Hoppy," I greeted, as I drifted by; I hooked his bicep and twitched a flipper to kick myself back in a loop his way.

"Having fun?" he smiled, wiping the water from his eyes.

"I think so." A deep and hearty chirr underscored the understatement.

A deer walked up to the edge of the pool, on delicate hind hooves and set them in the water.

Everything about her was diminutive. She was about 5'3, and all elegance and grace. Grey fur, with certain spots of white on the inner legs, with two large ears, with black tips, her face pulled into a long muzzle with black nose at the end.

Ricky swam up next to her and began talking. Predator and prey, it seemed surreal.

I saw Sonya exit the pool and seek a fluffy towel as I made my way up to the pair, curiosity building.

"You look great Mack," Ricky said.

A surprised yelp heralded my confusion.

"Mack?" The last time I saw her she was 6'3... and a guy.

She giggled.

"Never told you, did we?" She shared a conspiratorial glance with Ricky.

"Holy cow! Welcome to the other side sister." I spun around in the water, the long mystery that had begun that fateful night in the community center was finally solved.

"Thanks," she responded, shyly.

"Just about everything is set to go, as long as Ricky can get the ship started up next week," I reported.

"Sonya's been telling me all you've done. Really can't thank you enough. Took up right where I left off," Mack praised.

"I just chased the forms and tried to do what Sonya told me. You can never let the paperwork monsters rest, ya know," I mentioned.

"They are a terribly crafty bunch of buggers, indeed," the doe confirmed. An older man, dressed in trousers and a white shirt walked up and knelt down carefully next to Mack, avoiding the wet concrete.

"Mackenzie dear, is this the otter you speak of?" he asked in similar accent; come to think of it, he looked a lot like Mack once did.

"Yes sir. The very same. Got everything filed and underway," she praised.

I covered my small muzzle with my forepaws, embarrassed at the attention.

"I'd like to thank you personally for taking up this little project of my daughter's. The entrepreneurial spirit takes us in such interesting directions, but there's profit in all of it. You know, I'm very interested in this morphic business, would you mind taking some time to talk to my engineers?" he began to launch in a monologue.

"Papa, you promised, no work today," Mack complained and the older gentleman blushed.

"Sorry, yes, I suppose there will be plenty of time for that later." He rose, and kissed her between the ears. "Have fun sweetheart, I'll be along later, and welcome back."

"He seems great, you're really lucky," I commented.

"Yeah, he's still really confused, but he'll never show it, just tells me over and over. I had a crazy dream once too, chased it all the way through the atomic apocalypse and into a multi-billion credit company. If this is your dream, I'd be a hypocrite if I didn't let you take the same risks, so he mentored me, helped me with connections, but with the grant and all that, we had to bootstrap ourselves."

"Now it's all coming together. December 15th. You've done it Mack," I replied

"No, we've done, all of us. I got us started, you got us finished, with the help of everyone else on the committee. The reason we are getting out there, is because we all came together," she corrected.

"Like a family," I replied.

"Heck sweetheart, there's no 'like' about it, we are," Ricky replied.

"Exactly so," Mack agreed.

Chapter 25

I pulled the bedroom door closed. It was time.

It had been a year of change. Three moves, three cities, a new form. Today a new ship, and soon, a new planet.

Everything was happening in a blur.

"We need to get going, Aqua Girl." John called out from the front entrance.

"I know, I'm coming." I took a deep breath, and took one last look around.

Bounding out the front door, I began to move to the top of the ramp and then stopped, and reversed course.

"Forget something?" John asked, stopping his movement, thrusting his hand in his pocket, removing his keys just in case.

"This is it," I said. The words hung like a judge's sentence, as I looked around me. Taking in the cool near winter day.

Snow was already on the ground, and the evergreens were dusted with it. Taking a deep breath through my nostrils, I felt myself cool, as thousands of scents washed over me.

My last day on Earth. I wondered when I'd be back, if I'd ever come back.

Mom and Dad were on Mars and back to incommunicado. John was going to join me on Centioc.

What reason would there be to return?

The thought seemed odd. The reality began to click in.

After today, there would be a new sky, a new planet.

Goodbye, Earth.

A strange longing pulled at me as I moved up the ramp. Hopping into the co-pilot's seat, my usual exuberance was absent. Though it seemed a violation of my nature, I could not feel anything but solemn in that moment, reflective.

"Need some help belting in?" John asked.

"You know me," I replied, glad that he checked. He trusted me to do for myself.

My gaze returned back towards the window.

John finished buckling me in.

"This is Bluebird-775, requesting exit arc. Filing flight path," John radioed in.

"Cleared Bluebird, safe flight," Ground Control announced.

The craft began to alight as if gravity were an afterthought.

"You're strangely quiet," John mentioned, drawing me from my reflection.

"Weird day. Hard to know how to feel, solemn kind of." A whine escaped my throat as I considered my mood.

"I can understand that, another bombing at a clinic just yesterday, everything is just getting uglier." He wasn't helping.

"Will I ever be back John, do I even want to come back?" I asked.

"Well, who says you have to answer that question now? You're looking too far forward. Get out to Centioc, get started, see how it goes. Earth will still be here if you decide to come visit her," he encouraged.

"I am excited about that part. Can you imagine? Floating in an alien sea?" The sky darkened as the veil of the atmosphere parted, revealing a theater of stars.

"Can't really say I've ever thought about it like that, but I've never seen myself with flippers," he commented.

"There's hope for you yet. Life is better when you chitter," I replied, going for cheese.

"Oh God, please throw that back where it came from," he gagged dramatically.

We shared the laugh.

"How much longer till we dock?" I asked. He reached out with his left hand to a side console and entered a few commands.

"About forty five minutes more to her position. Danube is already in escort path," John reported.

"You hardly looked," I remarked .

"Like you knew exactly what your tail was doing when you were swimming the other day. Done it so much its instinct," he commented.

"Fair."

"This is what the bunny do," he continued.

"It's been a long time since I've heard you make a joke like that." It seemed like a good sign.

"Had a lot to think about lately, you and, well, Mack. Seeing her, as happy as she was," he said, flipping the automatic guidance switch and looking out the window, distracting himself.

This was a rare day.

"Hurting badly enough to talk or just kind of musing?" I asked; this was familiar territory for the both of us.

In that moment though, we were on two sides of it for the first time. He was, in a way, a shadow of my past, and, I hoped I was a portent of his future.

"Little of both. I've been here for a lot of your change. Can't help thinking I want it to be my turn. It's getting a lot harder to wait, a lot harder to ignore the hurt, ya know?" The conversation was like an old house, dusty and in disrepair. No matter how far I got from it, I had spent too much time here not to be familiar.

We drifted along.

"You've got a little over a year now before your enlistment is up; that's a perfect amount of time to plan and get set up. Why don't you call the realtor, talk about finally putting the Cabin on the market?" A craft, distantly ahead became visible, a ring ship, spinning in the night.

"It's a good idea, something to do while I'm escorting you fuzzies to your new home," he replied, showing greater conviction than I had seen from him in a long time.

"What's gotten into you?" I asked.

"I'm just tired. So fucking tired of it. It's here, and its time," he announced.

I reached out for him with my fore paw and he reached out and took it.

"I'm proud of you," I chirred.

He coughed and repositioned himself in the chair, working against the seat restraint.

"Excuse me," he said quickly.

"This is Bluebird-775 calling UEACS Hope, requesting docking clearance," John called out, switching to business.

"Heya John, I see you coming in there. Match our synchronization and bring her into the main bay." It was Kevin, already at his station.

"Roger that Hope, setting for guidance."

The Hope grew larger and the shuttle began to tilt into a spin.

It reminded me of a carnival ride.

Space whirled around and made me vaguely dizzy for a moment, but gradually, we came into a bay and glided down to a stop; everything seemed to right somewhat.

Weird.

Excitement raced through me and I fumbled with my harness, getting it free myself. Dashing through the tiny cabin like a reddish brown ribbon, I bounced at the edge of the ramp, waiting for it to lower, emitting a series of rhythmic chirps in time with the bouncing of forepaws.

"Easy. The ship has to last me back to the Danube," he chuckled, and let the ramp lower.

I slipped down and sniffed the air. Strange mechanical smells, the smell of sweat and old grease.

The grated floor hurt my flippers and paws.

John descended down and moved his head in a wide arc, taking it all in. A door at the far end of the Bay opened. Ricky and Sonya then entered in.

"Hi guys!" I chittered, bounding around them happily.

I looked back to John, as he quickly caught up.

"It's just like the old days," Ricky said, beaming with pride.

"You mean Noah's Ark?" John called out

We all fell to laughter.

"Stay for a tour?" Sonya asked.

"Really can't. Have an 'all hands' in a couple hours, pre-departure briefing," he explained

"Ever tell your commander all work and no play etc. etc.?" Ricky challenged, offering his paw out to John.

He took it in a firm handshake.

"Nah, I like being ranked above recruit." I rolled my eyes, as John turned to get underway.

"You two should date, I swear," I teased.

"Nah it's more fun being single and keeping my options open," John quipped back.

"Let's get you underway and settled in," Ricky said.

"Who am I rooming with?" I asked as we began to move towards the lift.

"Sonya, in officer's country, right near the bridge and sickbay," Ricky reported.

"I want to see sickbay as soon as possible," I said, hoping that my biggest issue would be band aids and aspirin medicine.

We reached the lift and Ricky jammed a button on the console.

"The doctor on the Danube wants you to check in with him tomorrow," Sonya reported. I would be practicing, and consulting with him over com channels. We would ship out anything serious.

"Any news yet when we'll get our own doctor?" I asked. The lift glided to a halt. We all filed out.

"They are still setting up the protocols for the training. UEA is promising us six months. In the meantime, we are going to be dealing with the military ships relaying in orbit." It was an imperfect system, but my license and training made it more tenable.

"Did you compile that list of people on board that have medical training for me?" I asked.

"Yep, waiting on your desk in the sickbay." That idea excited me.

"I have an office?" I chittered

"Part office, part closet," Ricky commented.

"I can't wait to see it," I replied.

"That's what I thought," Ricky answered. We came upon a wider than normal door, with a Medical caduceus painted down the middle, so that it split in half when it opened. Recognizing our presence through some kind of technical wizardry, the doors automatically slid open.

It had three semi-private Trauma bays. A room in the back was labeled, in black capital letters with the same caduceus emblem and SURGERY in bold black letters. Towards the back left corner was a very tiny room, with a desk built into the wall and a Chair fixed into the deck in front of it.

A surprise. On the nameplate, was my name; it read:

Joyce Coswell, BSN, Medic.

"You guys," I chittered happily

Boxes and crates of supplies filled two of the three bays. It was all up to me to arrange it and get unpacked.

It was clear I was going to be busy the next couple of days.

"Anything you need, just let me know," Ricky said.

"Oh this is going to be fun," I chirred, loving the feeling of a challenge.

Chapter 26

The day had finally arrived; we were about to make our first gate jump.

I had been busy in Sickbay the last few weeks, unpacking crates and setting things up. A few of the passengers had shown up to volunteer, which sped up the work rapidly.

The upper cabinet set mostly disused, and we had pulled out the documenting stations in the trauma Bays, setting up a table more to my standing proportions in the center where I could more easily coordinate. Utilizing that empty space, Ricky had taken some square crates and turned them so they opened out towards me, and rigged up two rows of shelving in each of them. They were just about my height, and so, the emergency and first aid supplies could be easily stacked and accessed if I needed them.

A high pierced whistled chirped twice, indicating a call from the bridge.

I hopped into my office and tapped the green button set into a console on the desk.

"This is sickbay, Go ahead," I announced, replying to the summons.

"Joyce, would you join us on the bridge? We need you at your station to get underway," Mack asked.

"Oh yeah, I'll be right there." UEA regulations required the senior medical official to be present on the bridge when the ship jumped. I thought briefly back to what John had said in the shuttle about Central Command and its ways.

Bounding over to the door, it slid open and I carefully made my way down the hall. The grates, a little harder on the flippers.

At the end of the hallway, tapping a panel, the doors swung open, revealing the bridge.

The large central screen was active. There was a hexagonal structured apparatus, drifting out against the black night of space. The Danube was just beside it.

Other ships dotted the sky, belonging to Central Command, and the press. The world had come to witness the jump of the first deep space colony.

The com chirped, drawing my focus from my station.

"This is the Danube bridge. We are prepared to jump. Upon successful completion, we will radio back then you will follow. Understood?" The militarily efficient nature flowed through the quipped tone and emotionless delivery.

"Roger that, Danube," Mack replied.

The Danube was there, followed by a brief flash, and it was gone.

The com chirped again. "Successful Jump. You are cleared to follow," the Danube reported from the ether.

Mack hit a button on her bridge console. "Ricky, how's the mechanics looking?"

"Everything's purring like a kitten down here. Let's spark her up," he said with pride.

"Confirmed."

"Kevin, if you would, please establish a connection to the Gate and transmit the codes," Mack ordered.

"Alright. Let me just punch them in here... Yep! That's it. Codes accepted." He reported.

Mack depressed another button inlaid into the armrest of the captain's chair.

"All hands, prepare for Jump. Prepare for Jump."

The world blinked away on the screen, an inky blackness, deeper than I had ever known, then a bright prismatic flash of white seemed to wash over the ship like a wave, and space had returned, but the stars were different, the patterns changed.

The lights flickered on the ship; there was a loud bang that seemed to rumble through the hull.

Gravity got weird, we started to float up.

I remembered my training, I remembered spinning.

I also remembered panic.

The click of a seat belt from Kevin's and Mack's chair had me fumbling for mine, as I drifted out of it.

Shit.

I swam back down, like I was back in the water and grasped on to the chair, changing my momentum and tying myself down as best I could.

"Engineering, status report," Mack called out.

Don't panic. Don't panic don't panic, I repeated in my head over and over.

The lights flickered back on and the ship began spinning again. The com chirped

"Danube bridge. Status report."

"This is the Hope, standby," Mack reported.

"Ricky, report," Mack ordered.

"Just a glitch in the power system after the jump. Popped half a dozen breakers down here. Will have to figure that out, but all the readings are fine," he reported.

"Just a minor anomaly with some of our systems Danube. We're fine," Mack reported.

I unclinched, and untied myself from the seat belt, with a relieved chirr.

We were now well on our way to Centioc.

Chapter 27

Hurry up, and wait.

Space travel, in a nutshell, is boring.

For the last month we had been underway, made our first jump and now everything was hum drum.

We still had a long way to go.

Life had settled down into a normal routine, consisting of a few hours spent in sickbay every morning in official capacity, followed by afternoons left largely to my own devices.

I hadn't had any customers, so I mainly played my function games and rearranged the supplies.

Hum-drum.

People knew where to go to get food. The ship had an entire library of entertainment media, and we were all eager to get started in Centioc One.

It meant that we had little to do.

The one exception was Ricky. The Hope was commissioned in 2047, and was showing her age.

I had never seen him happier.

"Bailing wire and duct tape, man. What did I tell you?" He flashed a grin, tightening down a quick repair to a leaking pipe in my quarters.

"That's about done it," he mentioned, rising, setting his tools back in the box.

"Thank you! Showers help me relax," I answered.

"Would have never guessed that. I have to get back to engineering," he mewed, and excused himself.

Using my tablet, I logged into the ship to see if anything pending or pressing was waiting.

My schedule was clear.

Pulling the chain, I ducked under the hot water, and nosed into the shower, imagining the alien seas of Centioc, drifting on my back in the water.

It was going to be heaven.

A half hour ticked by, and I decided to curl up with cartoons. Sonya checked in over the com.

"Hey, I've been kinda bored today, you want to have dinner tonight? We can start a new TV series," she offered.

"That sounds great. I'm not really doing anything here," I replied.

Another lazy afternoon. Cartoons lost my interest, so I distracted myself with function games instead.

An hour passed, another goal reached, another box checked.

A bored chitter followed. *Hum drum.*

General quarters sounded, sending an immediate strum of panic through me.

Making my way out of my quarters, I ran towards the bridge as hard as my flippers could take me.

I arrived just as I heard Ricky's terror-filled voice over the com.

"Mack, we have a problem! Big god-damned problem!"

"Calm down. Ricky, don't lose your head. What's going on?" she said. I took my station as my fear rose.

A low pitch whine highlighted my concern.

"I could smell it. I knew I could smell it, and now I can see it. I've got temperatures rising on the BEC-1. I think the initiator is destabilizing!" Oh shit, that did sound bad.

Sonya arrived, and took up an empty station, there for moral support. We were not a military crew. She reached out for my paw and I grasped hers as best I could. Mine was trembling.

So was hers.

"Kevin, raise the Danube," Mack ordered, the picture of calm.

"Danube-Bridge," came the efficient reply.

"We have a situation. Our Fission initiator may be destabilizing and is venting coolant, please notify your captain and prepare for evacuations," she relayed.

"Roger that. Keep us apprised, Danube out."

Twenty minutes ticked by like an agony. Ricky arrived, his fur covered in grease, reeking of sweat and fear.

"We are so... totally fucked," he announced.

"What's going on?" Mack pushed.

"Fission initiator is going into full meltdown. I'd say we have about two hours before it cascades. In that time, we are going to lose the temperature threshold for the BEC-1 and be limited to our batteries. But that's not the worst of it," he said, laying it all out.

"What's the worst of it?" Mack asked.

"We're all being irradiated. That smell, was the coolant fluid cooking off. The readings came in this morning confirming my worst fears."

"How long will the batteries last?"

"Has to maintain spin and life support, not much more than half an hour. We have to evacuate, and it's best we do it while we still have power."

"What about Centioc?" I pushed.

"Right now, without the Danube, we'd all be looking at our graves. Centioc is going to have to wait," he announced.

"We need to make it official. Call the mayday," Mack said.

"Kevin activate the distress beacon and open a channel to Danube bridge."

"Open," he said.

"Mayday-Mayday- This is the UEACS Hope calling for immediate evacuation. SOS. Repeat SOS. Our fission initiator is critical and at risk of runaway meltdown. We are taking radiation damage and venting coolant, repeat, we are taking radiation damage and venting coolant. SOS. SOS."

The main screen on board of the bridge activated to reveal the bridge crew of the Danube.

John was at his station in astrogation, looking out towards me worriedly.

"Yes, this is Captain Dougan, what can I do for you?" he said, not showing any concern or worry.

"We need your help. Our ship is damaged and won't survive. We have to evacuate the colonists," Mack explained, again.

"I'll take your request under advisement, I'll be back to you in thirty minutes," he answered, unconcerned, after which the com clicked off.

"What in the hell?" I was confused.

"He can't do that, it's not legal. Kevin get them back on the line," Sonya said.

"There's no response," he replied.

"Try them again, this is craziness," I begged.

"I am, all channels, they are ignoring us," Kevin answered, his long kangaroo rat tail swaying.

John... Please help me....

I didn't want to die. Not now, not like this.

"Ricky, is there anything you can do to buy us more time?" I asked.

A pained look went across his face as if he was doing terrible math. Finally, his shoulders sagged as if he had made some decision.

"Yeah. I'm heading back now. I'll keep things going as long as I can," he replied, then hugged Sonya and I.

"I'll join you. Joyce, you got us through when I was tanking. I'm going to leave you in command. Keep trying to raise the Danube. They're our only hope now," she announced.

"I'm not qualified to be a commander," I replied.

"You got us here. Ricky is going to need my help. Just keep them talking. I'll be right there on the com for anything over your head, as is Kevin at his station, and Ricky working next to me. You'll be fine," Mack quickly explained.

It did nothing for my confidence.

"I'll try. Don't go getting yourselves killed. We are going to get out of this." This was not where I was going to check out. I was going to make it. Swim in the bay of an alien planet.

I hadn't survived life in a human hell to die in space.

Thirty minutes ticked by, like clockwork, an incoming transmission request appeared, and was accepted.

"I'm sorry, but at this time, I can't risk my men to save a load of experiments," Dougan announced, his tone apathetic.

"This is murder!" John screamed, rising from his seat.

"Keep your seat lieutenant. Dial in a course. Take us away," he snapped.

"John! Please, captain, I'm begging you, there are 248 people aboard, we think, we feel. Please don't murder us. It's no risk yet. Just give us an hour. Let us get to the escape pods. Please I'm begging you." Panicked chitters, growls and yelps. Desperate pleas.

"This is a violation of our rights under UEA Charter. You have no right," Sonya screamed.

"I have a family coming after I get set up on Centioc," Kevin begged. "I have a little girl. Please don't make her an orphan."

"They're people god-dammit. Sir, this is beyond barbaric!" John again was on his feet.

"You stopped being people a long time ago anyway. Lieutenant Dawkins, lay in the course," he ordered.

"Sir I cannot follow that order. It is an illegal order," John reported, and stood by his station.

"Major Busker, draw your pistol and put it on the lieutenant," the captain ordered.

"No!" I screamed, shooting towards the screen in a futile gesture.

"Sir. I cannot follow that order. It is an illegal order," John said, again.

"Then you can die, and I'll step over your corpse and do it myself. I'm not going to let your little fetish get in the way of good men and good people," the captain said.

The major approached, and pressed the gun up to John's head; he pressed it more firmly into his temple, and then I saw the major whisper something into his ear.

John screamed, and went rigid. The major put his hand on John's and moved it towards the buttons, forcing him to input the commands. Finally, he came to the last switch. Again, he resisted. His face was a tortured agony. Finally, the major pressed hard with the pistol and screamed "DO IT"; John faltered, the final switch pressed.

"The Danube... is moving away, breaking from our position," Kevin reported.

Sonya broke down into tears.

"John, don't let this kill you. Don't let this stop you. Remember me, I love you..."

The line clicked off.

The lights began to flicker.

There was suddenly so little time left.

Twenty minutes ticked by.

Everything was fucked.

"Ricky, Mack, are you doing ok down there?" I called out from the bridge. The situation was deteriorating, the power was flickering and systems were out all over the ship; even the escape pods were haywire.

"No, sweetheart, I'm sorry. It's a losing battle. Fifteen minutes of power at most, but she's going hot. We're going to have to eject the core." Ricky delivered a death sentence.

There was no more denying it. We were at our end.

"Should we blow the ship?" Sonya asked, before continuing. "Seems better to go quick."

"No. We fight to the last. Never give up hope," I insisted. The rest of the committee nodded in agreement.

"The Danube could return. Ricky and Mack could work something out. Something could happen," I hoped.

It was all I had left.

"Fuck," Ricky reported, over the com.

"More problems?" It didn't seem like it could get any worse.

"I'm sorry. Know that we did the best we could," Mack said, his com went silent.

"Hey buddy, this is some straight up cowboy shit," Ricky said.

"Registering a manual core ejection," Kevin reported from a station.

"Oh God? Manual?" It sailed out into space on the monitor, and then detonated. The debris wave rocketed over the ship.

"Get them back on the line now," I ordered.

There was no response.

General quarters sounded.

"Alert--- Alert--- Main bulkheads in engineering have failed. Ship is venting atmosphere. Main Power failure in eight minutes. Evacuate. Evacuate.

Ricky and Mack were gone. The manual ejection procedure entailed venting that module into space.

That's why they had gone together. It took two people to pull the manual release.

It was a last ditch attempt to buy us time to save us all.

Eight minutes. Please let the Danube come back. Please.

"Alert--- Alert--- Main bulkheads in engineering have failed. Ship is venting atmosphere. Main Power failure in four minutes. Evacuate. Evacuate"

I held Sonya as she cried. Kevin joined me. We all huddled around the captain's chair.

A family, to the end.

Alert--- Alert--- Main bulkheads in engineering have failed. Ship is venting atmosphere. Main Power failure in two minutes. Evacuate. Evacuate.

I thought of the sea. I thought of hope. The sunrise.

Alert--- Alert--- Main bulkheads in engineering have failed. Ship is venting atmosphere. Main Power failure in one minutes. Evacuate. Evacuate

I thought of John and first loves.

The power went out.

The air started to get stale, and then, we all got sleepy.

In the end, I just drifted down. My last thoughts, of the ocean and home, and hope.

End of Joyce's Tale

John's Tale

Chapter 28

"You piece of shit!" Major Busker threw me from my seat but I did not care. Two security personnel took up position beside me.

"Take him into custody, but hold him here; I want Lieutenant Dawkins to see how this ends," Captain Dougan ordered with a sinister grin upon his face.

The Major's iron grip held me down, while I could think of nothing but killing both of them. I struggled and wiggled until my arms burned from his grasp.

"Why are you doing this? They're people god-dammit! You're murdering 250 people you monster!" A swift hard blow to the gut from the major followed my words, the first, no doubt, of many.

"Thank you major," Dougan replied.

The Danube registered a detonation.

She was... gone.

I screamed and pulled against the bonds and the two guards holding me; another wicked blow landed and I crumbled.

The sensation of being dragged, motion and movement. Light to dark to light.

Now in the brig, nothing mattered.

Hope was dead...

Everything was dead...

Don't let this kill you. Don't let this stop you. Remember me, I love...

Oh God, what had I done?

The door opened, bright light flooding into the dim space, the sound of boots.

"You god damn rat fucker. Putting us all at risk." Major Busker hauled me up and began working on my ribs.

"Fuck... you..." I replied, encouraging the beating.

I wanted to die. Hoped I would die.

Don't let this kill you. Don't let this stop you. Remember me.

The worlds rocketed through my memory; in her voice, like a heavenly mantra recited in the depths of hell.

Its light brought only pain. I wanted to beg for death. For the end.

Without relief or mercy, the words continued, as blows distantly fell.

Don't let this kill you. Don't let this stop you. Remember me.

How? How do I go on? Tell me my Angel, please have mercy on the damned.

Don't let this kill you. Don't let this stop you. Remember me.

But I was already dead. Everything I was, everything I thought I was died when I flipped the last switch.

He had forced every one, guided my hand through the movement I had practiced hundreds of times, except for the last.

Memories of the gun pressed to my temple, the feel of it, death standing, waiting for me, and then my cowardice.

Dead now. Just a shell, a remnant, still haunted and tortured by those terrible words.

Don't let this kill you. Don't let this stop you. Remember me.

It didn't make any sense. How... What was still alive inside of me?

"You piece of shit, are you even paying attention?" Another feeling of distant blows.

There was only one thing left to cherish.

Remember me.

There was only one thing within left to value...

Don't let this kill you.

But everything felt dead... What was left?

She had found her hope in change. I had watched her become a new person, envied her journey that I longed for myself.... I had envied her courage, that core value that I lacked, ultimately damning her by my cowardice.

Deep within, a tiny ember in a dark and frozen abyss sparked to a dull and angry red.

There was a chance I could still keep my promise.

Don't let this kill you. Don't let this stop you. Remember me.

Don't stop...

A command, an order, an instruction given.

Don't stop...

Her path... was still open.

If I lived.

I could walk it, follow it.

I didn't deserve it. It felt like profaning something sacred. How could I even dare to think?

Don't let this kill you. Don't let this stop you... Remember me.

It was the only way. I had no choice. There was only one way to honor her words, her love... her faith.

I had to change.

Chapter 29

One day bled into another. Nothing seemed to quite feel real anymore.

Numbness, unfeeling numbness and self-hatred. Deep, silent and complete.

The memory replaying over and over in tortured agony was part of every dream; every time I closed my eyes, there was that console, that fateful action.

My world had frozen into a deep and icy winter, as I sat in the brig, staring at the grey walls.

Unmoving, not eating. I was trying not to think, barely trying to be.

Only one thing kept me going. One thing kept me animated.

Her last request, my new foundation, my last hope.

Change.

The door slid open to reveal two ensigns from security.

"God he reeks," one said.

"Let's get him cleaned up and to his hearing," the other said.

Habits kicked in, lifetimes of routine. Shower, shave, uniform, boots. Salute, stand at attention; wait for a command.

I drifted by, watching as an observer as my body drifted on autopilot.

The captain entered, and I refused to salute, he did not press it. The major followed; a screen to our left lit up on the wall, revealing a two star admiral.

"Son, you've got a lot of charges you're facing. Insubordination, enticement to mutiny, failure to obey a direct order. There's enough here to put you in Ort 13 for the next fifty years," he said, trying to intimidate me.

I remained silent.

"So here's the deal. You take an Honorable, and we quietly let you off back at Earth. You go your way, we go ours, provided you keep your mouth shut."

They wanted this to go away, and they weren't spacing me. Half-starved and swimming in grief, it took a moment for the connections to fire.

First Contact team. Mack's father. The Mendians. The mission.

They needed me to go quietly. I was just enough of a 'somebody' to be a problem. They were trying to make this go way.

"I want to shift with Dr. Andropov as soon as I get back to Earth. Cut me an honorable and guarantee me passage to Centioc and we have a deal," I replied.

"You got some balls you little shit," Captain Dougan rose in protest.

Apathy flashed to a quick and hidden anger.

"I've got some balls, after you just murdered 250 people and my best fucking friend, you bastard. You haven't spaced me because you can't. Just a little too much attention on the both of us, isn't there, so how about you shut the fuck up and take it like the bitch you are?"

The captain's hand contracted into a fist, and I was certain he was going to attack me in front of the admiral.

"As you were captain," the admiral shouted, as Dougan rose. As if on an invisible leash, he sat back down.

"You want to shift, and be exiled to an alien world with no communication? I want to be very clear about this," the admiral asked.

"That's all I want," I confirmed.

His eyes lit up with the possibilities of one of the First Contact team taking up the Mendian Path of The Other.

"Oh, I think that can be arranged," he replied.

Chapter 30

My time in the military was over; boarding a civilian transport from Central Command, with my duffel bag slung over my shoulder, I was slowly learning how to live again, to fake the motions of being a living person.

Still though, I felt like a zombie marooned in the land of living. Every time I slept, there was still only that one dream. Over and over.

Every night. I saw her face, her ghost, spurring me on.

The cabin was going on the market. I needed the money for a shuttle. My appointment with Andropov was for the 28th of February. All my paperwork had been submitted from the Danube.

There was no excitement, only path and a firm need to destroy everything in me that had ever flipped that switch. What I had yearned for my entire life, hoped for in desperate wanting as the years only fed my desperation, had finally come in frozen winter, and I could not feel any of it. It was salvation, the need deeper than it had ever been, but the joy of achieving it, like so many other emotions, was gone...

I didn't need them; I only needed to survive, to rip out the heart of the bastard that had killed her.

There was nothing to do. No reason to even visit her "grave". There was no point. Her parents sent me the video of her memorial, and never once did they mention the otter she was, just the human she wasn't.

They had buried the shadow of their daughter. I had damned her substance.

Everything seemed meaningless and bleak. Only one thing seemed to have value.

The one thing that had given me meaning my entire life, the one thing that I had left that still lived and breathed in this world.

The Hare.

Finding Joyce had been a godsend. Someone who understood, who wasn't just a distant voice on a screen or a message board.

She could see me, the only one that ever had. The always-present human lie was no barrier.

Like the angel she was, she knew only truth.

I had spent my teenage years and my twenties wandering in and out of the various net communities, but I had never found a home there, but Joyce, she was special.

My confessor and my support. She believed in me when everyone else hadn't and helped me through my dad dying.

And then I...

Fuck.

Her last request, that I honor that last living thing. The glowing ember in my world, quietly shedding its light.

February 28th, 2073. For you Joyce, for what you always wanted for me.

May I come out better than the fiend that killed you.

An intense need for the change. The tank most of all, the idea of seven months asleep, away from this hell, away from my memories. I hoped. The chance to be something other than *this.*

It had been with me throughout life, but this was new, a burning urgency. Desperation fueled by the weight of my sin. It was not just my rebirth in that moment, it was my redemption.

I could be a new creature that would never be a coward again, never turn my back again. My values could be her values, joy, hope, faith.

It was a terrible juxtaposition, of wanting to feel joy, of knowing this is all you've ever wanted, but so much had changed. It was the last thing left, all I had, all I had ever had, besides her.

From that small foundation, I had to rebuild, had to find some way forward.

There was no energy within me for it. The idea of laying down in the cabin and just waiting, waiting for my body to fail and death to surround me competed with my mission.

It would be so easy just to let it slip. I had tried before. It was my deepest secret. The memories of how the blood felt as it flowed from the wound on my wrist, the coolness at the tips of the fingers, as the red liquid pooled over the sink. There was a twisted hope that came through the ragged burning that this was finally the end, that there would be no pain.

It would be so easy to feel that warped kind of joy again. The relief of it all. I remember the black conceits it whispered. It was ending, finally done; finally free.

Just another lie. I had survived, made excuses, said nothing.

Like what you always do.

The emotion surged, and angry tears fell. Embarrassment surged that I was in public.

No more excuses. No more easy ways. Truth, John. Nothing but truth. You lost all right to lie when you killed her.

"Saw some shit, eh buddy? Been there," said an older man sitting in the window seat of the transport. He was of a soldiers cut, smiling he leaned over and patted my shoulder in a gesture of support.

"Could say that," I replied, feeling embarrassed.

Mercifully, he left me in silence as the craft descended.

Another blur of travel. Transfers, my bag cutting into my shoulder; wanting only quiet and time away from the concrete human hive that surrounded me.

Finally, exhausted, sliding the key into the lock of the cabin, the door opened and the lights flickered on to reveal a stack of tuna cans along the wall.

It hit me as if it was a crowbar; I collapsed in a heap in the floor and lost it, wailing in pain and agony.

The cabin felt haunted. Reminders of her seemed to be everywhere. A bit of fur. A stack of empty cans, neatly stacked in the bathroom trash can.

Then her ghost appeared.

Opening the bedroom door, we had neglected to make the bed, and the small nest of blankets she had made around her, was still there, along with the otter plush I had given her.

There was note with it. *Don't give up. You'll get there.*

I clutched it tight to my chest and held it, never wanting to let it go, laying down next to the spot in the blankets carefully, and wishing for blackness that finally came.

Chapter 31

The routine.

Eyes snap open.

Immediate feeling of shock, confusion, regret.

Awareness pulls vaguely downward. From panic to despair.

Another day.

Memories; that moment of full awareness that descends.

The knife through the chest.

Oh God, another morning, another day like this.

Anger, frustration, pain.

My morning routine, my entire life, now punctuated by the fires of grief and agony.

I suppose these things happen.

Coffee and toast. Sit on the couch. Stare at the screen.

Vaguely, I was aware of my heart beating.

My tablet vibrated, an appointment reminder. Thirty-two missed requests for contact.

How had it been five days already?

Time was one of the many things that no longer felt real.

The press didn't want to leave me alone. They smelled a story and had hovered at the edges of my property like buzzing flies over a rotting corpse.

Still, I remained a sphinx-like riddle, no statements made; no appearances given. I had sold my voice, and my chance for revenge for something better.

Hope.

Rhythms, for time immemorial, my life had seemed lost to rhythms. Moving about the cabin like a ghost this last week, I distracted myself, numbly moving things into boxes and setting things away.

The place became sparse and empty, much like how I felt within. Everything off to the landfill or storage.

I had no will for such tasks and moved through it like a zombie, but my directive remained, and I had to fulfill it, so I had to be ready.

No more excuses; just focus on the goal. This place was familiar, the numbness the cold.

Survival training, UEA Camp Winter, deep in Siberia, four weeks in the snow.

Three days without food, fingers numb, on the edge of exposure. Everything had switched off to a distant numbness as the orders flowed and robotic obedience ensued. It was the only thing left. Reason destroyed by the extremes, my brain working only by training.

And here we were again, now lost in deeper winter; no reason to think, just next steps. Focus on what you need to do.

Pack up the Cabin. Check

Eat something. Check.

Don't stop....

In spite of the numbness, the last one proved an icy hill. I struggled, I slipped, I flailed, crawling over it in a desperate need to go forward.

Frozen, cut and bleeding, pushing through the snows, thinking only of the goal.

The mattress was now on the floor in an otherwise empty room. Low shelves along one barren wall for food. Ration bars, mainly. They were cheap, and I didn't give a shit about the irony. The cabin, stripped of all reminders, stripped of everything but quiet.

Barrenness.

Winter.

Oh how I longed for the winter, even though it was here.

The cabin, no longer my fathers.

Now, it was my cell.

It was what I needed. Cleanness... Bleakness.

Time to think... To process... to be.

But not today.

It was the 28th, and I had somewhere to be.

The challenge terrified me, of existing as more than a shadow, of being more than a ghost that packed cabins and waited for fate.

Fate had come, and with it, the desperate rise towards solidity.

In almost a flash, it seemed as if I was transported. The morning melted in a blur, compact with the sounds and smells of public transport, the bump and arc of orbital travel.

Suddenly a new place. *The Hague.*

United Earth Medical Center.

In spite of my mourning, it was already time for last things.

Chapter 32

"Sit down my boy, we will get underway," Andropov motioned to a chair across from an ancient metal desk, set into the corner of his tiny office, deep on the second subterranean level of the United Earth Medical Center.

I nodded, and sat down in my seat quietly.

"Alright, so you are already somewhat familiar with the process," the doctor reported; a bracelet was lying open on his desk with a key next to it, sat on a pad connected to his terminal.

"Yes. I was around for much of Joyce's change." The mention of her name sent a surge of feeling through the icy bands of numbness that seemed to surround me.

"Indeed. So down to business." He opened a drawer and removed a clipboard tablet.

"Let's see, now you understand, that this process will be permanent for at least three years, correct? There is no stopping once you've begun." he asked.

"Yes." Same old rigmarole.

"And you understand that this is to shift your physical form to a *female* Snowshoe Hare, *feral*." I noticed the emphasis on the two words.

"Yes." A distant sense of shame from a lifetime of training burned distantly in my frosted night. It seemed alien being so direct about a truth I had always hid.

"That will not be a problem, do you have a specific name in mind? I've not yet pushed the final configuration to your bracelet," he replied; much of the clinical nature he had shown when I had seen him around Joyce seemed relaxed, if only slightly.

"Snow," I replied. The name, a relic from my childhood. My hours of playing pretend, of dreaming of a body that was mine. Even then, it tore at me, but there was always hope in play.

Whenever I wanted, I could be Snow.

There had come a time when life forced me to put those things away, to bury those childish conceits deep, informed by those around me, and their cruelties, their expectations.

The world, however, had turned. Now it was time to put their lies away; the rote method I had talked, and walked, like a religious acolyte my entire life, informing me how to be-ended today.

There was no better name. The last relic of my innocence, the memories of its distant hope. What could be more appropriate?

The doctor tapped a few keys into his keyboard and the bracelet vibrated on the pad.

Just like that.

"Ok, now, do you want to stop? Last chance."

I shook my head, and he lifted the bracelet off the pad, and locked it around my left wrist.

"S. Dawkins." Showed on a tiny display above the silhouette of a hare.

"One more thing. Let us violate protocol a little bit." He shut his door, mysteriously and opened a drawer, drawing out a bottle of vodka, with two glasses.

He poured a small amount in each, and handed one to me.

"Do not worry about your shift. The nanites are unstoppable and relentless. Trust me. You will feel like garbage in forty-five minutes regardless. As for me, I do not normally do this, but for the dead, da? The little vydra, may God rest her soul."

The doctor raised his glass, and drank, then quickly popped a breath mint and secreted the bottles away.

It seemed a little too familiar to be spontaneous, but in that moment, I didn't care. We were all haunted by our ghosts, damned by our demons; we made our ways the best we could.

Ritual over, and dead honored, he walked me out to the strange green recliner like chairs where I would begin.

New rhythms. IVs dropped, bags hung and then more waiting.

Hurry up, and wait. Some things never changed.

Forty-five minutes hit, and like clockwork, I was sick. Everything contracted and my guts spasmed so hard my back cracked.

The month of fun, had begun.

Chapter 33

Everything was changing. Some things were gone and others remained. Life had found a way to become even stranger.

Mood swings. Oh God, the mood swings. Joy, to anger, to despair and then everything was suddenly beautiful again, competing with my grief, switching on and off like a light switch. Leaving me with feelings akin to a type of emotional whiplash.

Thirty minutes weeping over a commercial about nursing homes.

Fuck, Snow, pull yourself together.

A wave of nausea, followed by the inevitable vomiting centered me.

That's right. Paperwork. That's what I was doing before being assaulted by the people selling the abandonment of relatives at affordable prices.

They even had shuffleboard. *Joy*

My unwilling skeleton creaked as I shifted myself in my seat, and got back to work. I had to get this in today.

My first month had passed in a blur of sickness and grief, but as the changes manifested, and the world around me slowly began to pull itself from the icy grip of winter, something began to live in me.

I both loved, and hated it.

It was life. Joy. Every day, I saw the hare a little more, and John a little less, but still the memories waited, every night when I slept, I damned Joyce over and over again.

Each morning, I arose as one of the guilty. Only in my change did I find any redemption.

A deep burning anger that I had always known, had died, faded and gone silent. Its absence left a ringing in my soul that seemed to persist for days after the event happened. Ancient pains, and agonies were slowly falling quiet, as my body contorted violently in the throes of its changes.

In all of the chaos, and the pain, it began to separate me from my grief. Still foundational, like a cornerstone in my world, it became distant, as new things grew from the barren soils of my soul.

Life, brought to you by Shift Tech.

A new shame though... like the sting left over from the burn...

I felt so unworthy of all of it, of them and their legacy.

Not just Joyce, the entire two hundred and forty-eight had all pioneered and persevered while I watched and made excuses.

Every night I wished for the chance to go back, just so I could die with them, a new ritual, replacing the old prayers for change.

Change had come, and far too late, but I had earned this curse, and it was now my duty to carry on.

"Booster, booster," my bracelet vibrated; grabbing my cane, I hobbled my way into the kitchen, and went through my rhythms. I was having considerable more locomotion problems than Joyce at this early stage. My hips and knees just did not want to function right anymore.

Stopping to catch my breath from all the activity of movement, my tablet began to chime and vibrate again in the other room.

No rest for the wicked.

Hobbling back the other way, my skeleton protesting every movement, vaguely hunched, leaning over my cane, feeling closer to ninety than thirty in that moment, I took a deep breath and centered myself against the growing feelings of anxiety and panic as the rapid fire events crashed around me.

Paperwork, booster alerts.... my thoughts cascaded from one thing to another as my chest tightened.

Easy... I said to myself... *Easy.*

The world resolved again to sense around me, as I checked the notification.

'Appointment reminder, court house, name change/tags,' it read from my calendar.

My eyes shifted down to the half completed form, and the rapidly dwindling time.

Fuck.

Setting down to work with shaky affect, I was making good progress when my tablet again erupted into a sea of noise, causing me to leap out of my spot.

It was a regretted action immediately. Hips popped, knees popped and feet popped, as tiny burning rivulets of pain raced up and down my lower skeleton and I fell hard onto the ground.

The tablet, now next to my head, was incessantly ringing, contributing to a headache.

Remember you deserve this. I reminded myself, and answered the call.

"Dawkins," I responded, half dead.

"Yes, this is Caroline Meyers, your real estate agent. We've got a bite on the cabin, but it has to be tomorrow, can we do a showing then?" she asked.

It was getting down to crunch time; I only had a few weeks before the tank. Sooner really was better.

The cabin was mostly empty, but still needed a cleaning; and in my state, that would take all night, if I didn't get sick.

"Mr. Dawkins, are you there?" she asked.

"Yes, yes, that will be fine," I replied, committing to the impossible.

"Great, just make sure it's show ready. Presentation is everything," she reminded.

My gaze fell to the open, emptied cabinets in the kitchen, the pile of trash in the corner and the dust that seemed to be everywhere.

Fuck.

"Oh, it will be just great. I assure you," I replied, damning myself.

The line clicked and fell silent.

Tears. They seemed to come constantly, a general tool of emotional expression.

I wondered how much longer they would persist.

The floor was hard and unforgiving, but supportive; moreover, the numb burning in my skeleton made it vaguely comfortable.

Just gonna lie here for a bit.

A flash of blackness ensued... then a piercing noise. Startling awake, I again jostled my abused frame.

Appointment- Name Change/Tags 2 hours.

I had lost more time. Dragging myself to my cane, I hoisted myself up to get ready.

Chapter 34

Another two weeks, more changes. Fur and whiskers. Sixty pounds down. My eyes now brownish black. My ears pointed.

I could no longer deny, in any way, that I was becoming a new creature. I felt like a new creature.

At first, it had seemed such an impossible conceit, but one morning amidst the pain, and the grief, I awoke, and there had not been that same dream, that same awful dream.

No. That night, there was a new dream of freedom, of joy; and I still yearned for it even now, hours after it had finished. Then I reflected on it by the firelight, as if I had suddenly, in some way discovered sunrise after an eternity of night.

Joyous, sweet rapture, wholeness... almost like I was experiencing these emotions for the first time, discovering them, after a lifetime frozen in a block of ice.

I felt a type of manic ecstasy, everything vibrating in truth, and in love. I was overwhelmed with it, and could not cry; the process too far along now, but I did not care.

Everything... I had everything I had ever wanted right in front of me.

The dream was so simple. A warm summer's day, a tall grassy field, thousands of scents, some inspiring hunger, others- caution. Information came streaming in from my world from all corners.

My whiskers twitched in subtle breeze, as there was the sound of songbirds in varying patches of volume and concentration, immersed and lost in tracking the million subtle beauties of the world.

It felt good just to sit and watch everything, observe everything, revel in it all from quiet distance, and then out of nowhere, the impulse to run.

The thought of flying through the grass, stalks whipping by, striking my whiskers and making my muzzle twitch; darting in and out, as paws tore into dirt, gaining and finding their traction.

Elation. Freedom...

No *Hope* burning in the depths of space...

That one thought had shattered the illusion, tainted it, sending it violently out of control, forcing me awake. My sheets were soaked; I was gasping.

For all the sadness I had felt, for the first time, the joy was stronger, which built, unexpectedly into a tsunami of shame.

It felt like such a sin to forget, even for a moment, but the relief was heaven sent, and desperately needed.

Even its memory brought gasping, as if coming to fresh air, of finding life from the impossible frozen abyss of death.

The last six weeks a blur; canes and voice collars, changing proportions and perspectives. The cabin was under contract and sold for all intents and purposes. Life had come and gone so fast.

Life in many ways, had begun again.

Strange reflective thoughts ensued. I shifted by the fire and the tags from my voice collar jingled some.

My hips hurt constantly, and I could barely walk. A low strum of excitement rippled through my chest, keeping me at a high and manic edge.

Tanking would commence, tomorrow.

I was supposed to be asleep, resting up for the seven months of rest that awaited me. Instead, hot tea by the fire, my last night as anything close to human. I decided to keep vigil over the final hours, observing every second, when all I wanted was for the hours to melt away.

Still recovering from that wonderful dream, it warred against my grief, which now lived at the edges. There was a growing comfort with the loss. Not a resolution, not a patch, not a scar; just an acceptance of the hole left behind by her absence.

It had all become familiar, part of the routine and so new joys competed with the old pains that were, what they were.

As strange as it was, I just didn't feel like him anymore. I don't know when it happened, but one day "John" existed as a type of connected shadow, as if I was the inheritor of his guilt and his sins. My purpose now, was to carry it, to seek the redemption of our shared soul.

Even before tanking, something new was emerging out of the cabin in the Kelowna woods.

The time passed by like a slow agony. Memories of Joyce, bringing a kind of sad and mournful nostalgia.

I pulled her otter plush close; it had been my constant companion through my shift so far. It still smelled like her, at the edges. My changes, bringing that to a full and present awareness.

Every time I held it, it was almost like she was there with me. Unbidden, her last words drifted across my memories.

Don't let this kill you. Don't let this stop you. Remember me.

For you Joyce. For hope.

A stubborn wave of fatigue washed over me. Warm by the fire, covered in a blanket, the world grew fuzzy at the edges, as my head drifted down.

Time passed.

The sound of birds drifted vaguely at the edge of my awareness and my eyes snapped open. The fire had died, my tea cold. Two hours had drifted by on the clock.

Here, the sun was rising.

In a blur, the morning faded into familiar pains and rhythms, as I drifted through them in surreal fog. My transport would be here in half an hour; the realtor had the key.

Before I knew it, I was back at United Earth Medical Center, standing in front of my tank.

"Voice collar," Dr. Andropov reminded. With fumbling paws in mid-shift, I struggled with the clasp. I got lucky, and it gave way quickly.

"Alright Snow, up and onto the bed." He patted it with his left hand.

"It's the big day, I know. Will not take long," he said, I felt a vague pin prick, then another. The world began to get hazy.

"Drifty now, is nice da?" he asked, but distant now... that strange cold numbness radiating up from my arm and then...

Blackness...

Deep, whole and complete.

Strange memories, flitting by, a different life, a better life. The painful one growing further and further away.

There was a field... a place to run, a place to graze...

Freedom... Long days of hyper vigilance. Anxiety, one day a loud noise... Strange pain...

However, briefly, there was a new place, strange smells. Acrid. Bizarre two legged creatures that left food in blocks.

Suddenly, there was green grass again, a safer place. Still, strange two-leggers with the food blocks. All is routine, all is well. Some of the two leggers had rectangles that flashed with lights sometimes.

Peace. Finally. Peace

Sinking deeply into it, wanting nothing but that, everything else was far, away. Run, graze, groom sleep.

Things that mattered. Rhythms... patterns... routines.

Just be.

Time passed. Seasons changed in the strange memories.

The sun rose and with it, an urgency. Brightness, the world growing whiter, building to a high crescendo.

Chapter 35

My eyes snapped open in the tank.

My left fore paw floated in my vision; lines and wires were connected to me. I could feel a mask over my muzzle, the world strangely distorted by the viscous liquid I was floating in.

A light beamed in from the top, as someone gently lifts me out. Then the feeling of a warm, fluffy towel.

Comfort... A nap for a moment...

So tired. Ironic considering I just slept for seven months.

"Snow? Snow?" Dr. Andropov prodded, setting my collar down next to me. It was purple, and had my morphic identifier tags; slipping it on, it connected to the bots in my system.

Everything about my body felt new, but also familiar. Flexing my squat forepaws, I reached out and dug into the fabric of the bed I was perched on and pulled forward in a stretch, my hind paws pushing back as my back lengthened with a pop.

"Are you ok?" he asked.

"Overwhelmed." It was crashing into me like waves. Everything tingled; I wanted nothing else but to run for the pure joy of it, the elation.

A drive built in me and I kicked in a high leap up off the bed and then twisted my body, landing back down on the end: the movement, an expression of ecstasy.

No more pain. No more lie.

"It's not a dream," I reported.

"No, not a dream at all, but we do need to have a discussion. I need to you to focus Snow."

"I'm a hare." The doctor rolled his eyes and smiled, having been down this road many times.

"Lepus Americanus. Huge hind paws." He sat down next to me on the bed.

"Are you feeling ok? No issues, no neural glitches?" he checked.

"I feel, incredible. Me, for the first time. Hi doc. It's nice to meet you again," It felt cheesy to say it that way, but I couldn't help it. A strange kind of happiness I had never known drove me to sentimentality. In that moment, I loved everything, felt joy for everything and could feel nothing else in that moment.

Freedom, after a lifetime of darkness. Freedom, after a lifetime of lies.

I had done it. I'd become the Hare. I was half way through keeping my promises.

"It's nice to meet you too miss. Now, can you tell me your name?" he asked.

"Snow Dawkins," I replied with pride.

"And where are you?"

"United Earth Medical Center." The scent gave it away as much as the decor.

"Who's the chancellor?" he pushed.

"Well, when I tanked it was Vicki Gomez, but she was in hot water. I figure general election has been called by now," I replied.

He chuckled. "George Parker is the new one. You are fine. A few days in observation and then you will be released."

He patted my head and rose. In the corner was a small box with my belongings.

My old clothes. They were no longer in any way made for my body or proportions. Now I was 1.2 meters long, if you counted my ears and firmly a quadruped. There was no longer any place in my life for jogging pants.

In a strange type of farewell ceremony, I dropped the old clothes in the trash bin and nosed into my bag. There was my new harness I had ordered with its side bags attached, my tablet and Joyce's otter plush.

Joyce. An immediate feeling of guilt rammed its way into my happy world, as the realization dawned that I had not thought of her to this point. The scents from the toy washed over me. I clung to it, holding it tighter; its presence and existence somehow granting me comfort from my grief. In some way, it was like she was still here with me.

Memories of her exuberance out of the tank. *Look at me, I'm an otter, I'm an otter!*

In that moment, I would have given anything for just five more minutes with her. One last chance to show her I was free, and keeping my promise.

But even in a time of miracles, the most earnest prayers often go answered.

Chapter 36

Two days had passed, and I was about to be released from observation. My harness was on, causing hotspots in my fur. It proudly proclaimed my sentience for all to see.

A familiar demon walked into my hospital room. The admiral from my brief hearing on the Danube, now live and in person.

"You've got a promise to keep lieutenant, and a ship to catch," he said, without preamble.

I realized in that moment, he had never introduced himself, not even on the ship. Just a vague specter of authority to make deals with or cajole. Scanning his uniform, I found his nameplate.

1. McGregor.

"Going to need a shuttle, or its going to be awfully difficult." If he wanted to dance, we would dance.

"What are you doing about that?" he shifted, going direct.

"For the last seven months or so, not much, mainly sleeping," I replied and drummed a hind paw for emphasis.

"The UEA is currently auctioning off some retrofitted models from the 2040s and 2050s. They may work for your purposes." He handed over a tablet. "This also has your packet for re-certification, everything you need."

"A retrofitted shuttle is not going to get me out to Centioc alone." They had no gate drive, it would be an absurdly long trip.

"Check your tablet, lieutenant. You've got a spot as cargo on the Masamune in February. That's your deadline, February 16th, one way or another you are going to be on the ship that day. I suggest you get ready because this is the end of my involvement." He turned and walked out.

"Aw, your concern is so overwhelming I thought I'd ask you to dinner," I said, raising my voice through the collar some to make sure he heard me on his way out.

Asshat.

Waiting for my discharge papers, I pulled up the listing catalog he had left of UEA shuttles for sale. One in particular caught my eye.

It was ancient, from 2040. A deep space scout class Gen 1 Shuttle; it had a relatively new fusion reactor, but was otherwise as old as dirt, twice retrofitted, but a look at the interior showed the true appeal of the design.

They built it as one big room with a small bathroom tucked into the back right corner of the ship. Two bunks were set into the wall on one side, but the pilot's seat and controls were all switches and joysticks. The shower, designed for microgravity, operated on a pull chain.

The shuttle was spartan, but it would be easy to modify for my challenges with human design. It was also tough as hell, overbuilt from an era when the paranoia of what might be out there, and the potential distance from help, dominated. Thus, they were made for reliability and durability to the utter and unassailable limits of the lowest bidder design of its day.

It seemed perfect, until I checked the price.... 85,000 credits, I only had 110,000 after liquidating everything.

Pulling out my own tablet from beside me, its more capable cousin, I ran some numbers. I needed food to get me out there; there would be registration fees, I needed some place to live, or park it in the interim, as well as fuel, maintenance, modification, taxes and title fees.

My once thought to be sizable nest egg, dwindled before my eyes, leaving me with five k to live on for the next two months, barring emergencies or surprises with the shuttle.

If I even got that shuttle... *Were there any cheaper?*

A quick scan dashed my hopes, showing nothing comparable in the range, and the private market, I knew, was even worse; they were a high demand item.

Suddenly, my best hopes of escape, and perhaps my last, rode on one pony. I eagerly tapped the button to schedule an inquiry for sale.

No pressure.

With that crisis now simmering on the back burner, another more pressing concern presented itself.

Where was I going to go?

The cabin was gone, and my friends were mainly relegated to the military. My life had been one of distant connections with rare exception.

Mom? Ha! I quickly chucked that idea. Two months in the grass watching for hawks would be better than that.

Once I had the shuttle, I could park it anywhere. I could even find an empty patch of land, after I had it stocked and just exist out of it.

Something the admiral said though went through my mind... I checked back through the files on the cheap data tablet he had brought to ferry files, and found a re-certification packet.

Damn.

No camp out for me; I couldn't even fly the damn thing until I completed a battery of tests at a local spaceport to determine my ability to operate craft.

A rock and a hard place. If I somehow didn't pass re-certification, how would I get to Centioc, what would be done then?

I really didn't want to find out. A chill of fear strummed through my hind paws and I had to re-center. Focus Snow. One thing at a time; there will be plenty of time to freak out later.

This was just more bullshit to hop through.

Checking the schedule, my options soon became clear. The module was three weeks long, I had to provide the shuttle, and five cities were listed with currently active courses.

San Francisco, Sydney, Tokyo, Omaha, Johannesburg or The Hague.

When they put it that way, the choice was easy.

Chapter 37

"Ladies and Gentleman, this is your captain speaking; we are on final approach into San Francisco International Spaceport, it's a balmy sixteen degrees. We'd like to wish you all a very happy holiday season, and a Merry Christmas if you celebrate it. Thank you for flying United Earth Spacelines."

A stewardess drifted by and checked to make sure I was still belted in. A harness that buckled at my chest, hung a bit heavy there, causing a vague protest from my back over the brief two hour jaunt through security and terminals on my way back to good ol' North America, Sector Two.

Of all the cities I had to choose from on my packet, this was the one most familiar. It also, reminded me of her. If I was to be marooned here for two months, it seemed better to dwell where my ghosts would be comfortable.

A woman sat rigidly in the seat next to me, staring straight ahead, having hardly said a word the entire flight. Upon emerging from the tank, it seemed the world had gone to sudden and great lengths to show me how different my reality now was.

The city grew larger from my perch, as I gazed out the window, and soon, there was a familiar thud and we were down. The craft alighted on its pad as the spaceway rolled up to the hatch, attaching with the familiar sound of two locking bolts.

The lights drew up in the cabin, and everyone rose. I remained in my seat, content to wait until the transport had cleared a bit.

The smell of eagerness and human sweat punctuated the air in acrid tones, mixed with vague hints of both stress and fear. It contributed to my own building panic, feeling surrounded by predators, and all I wanted in that moment was out.

Slowly, the two-leggers filed by. *Geeze, please hurry up people.* I fumbled with the latch of my seat belt harness and wiggled it free.

"Aww, what a cute bunny, where's your owner?" A random woman asked, and stroked my ears, ignoring my harness, and HUMAN EQUIVALENT INTELLIGENCE stenciled in large red and yellow letters down my sides.

"I was good and they gave me my freedom papers. Snow is no longer a slave to the furless authorities!" I proclaimed through my collar with sarcasm and she jerked back in surprise.

"I'm... I'm sorry," she gasped and quickly made her way off the craft.

The stewardess, chuckling to herself, quickly came to check on me.

"Everything alright miss?" Everyone just seemed to naturally assume I was a female now, which for me was new; was it my species? My voice certainly sounded the part, though with focus, I had some degree of control of that through my collar.

It all had to do with thinking in a different tone of voice from your inner monologue. It was imperfect, but sometimes I could make it work.

And for my next trick...

"Yes, I'm fine thank you. Just with my size, it's better to avoid the stomping feet." I was learning quickly to watch where I stepped, because no one was watching out for me.

With the craft empty, I finally made my way out; bounding down the corridor, the flight crew following just behind.

My world opened out onto the space port concourse.

"Bunny!" I heard a young girl call out.

Forget this. I took off in a run down the concourse, not too fast, but enough to avoid people. Using my size and reflexes to move around quickly and efficiently, I was nearing the checkpoint up ahead when a guard yelled for me to slow down.

Begrudgingly I slowed to a hop.

"Sorry," I replied.

My induction into my new reality continued as I made my way on to the escalator, for the final ride up to the platform for the Bay Area Rapid Transit System, or BART. A banner was strung up in the terminal that read.

BART 1972-2072, Celebrating 100 years.

Moving up to the turn style, I found I couldn't reach the scanner with my tablet without hopping. My forelegs only moved so far. An attendant approached and helped me scan through.

"Move it freak," a fellow passenger bumped into me rudely, as I went to thank the attendant.

I had been out of the hospital four hours and already, it felt like a long day.

Chapter 38

Flight re-certification, as a morphic, is a giant pain in the ass.

I was quickly working my way through my first week. Reflex checks and physicals 'ad nauseam'.

In all the hustle and bustle, one thing had slipped through the cracks, and I was now paying for it, in a new kind of agony.

I had forgotten my flea treatment; I was infested at the moment, and itching like mad.

It was costing one of my three, allowed, medical exemption days, but I had to take it. The little jerks were voracious and would not leave me alone.

As if to punctuate the thought, an intense twinge from my ear erupted into full and desperate need.

"Gah! Son of a bitch!" I cried and rapidly attacked the spot with my hind paw, bringing only temporary relief.

Why Snow, why had you forgotten your flea treatment?

Desperate for relief, I dialed the name of an organization I found online, something I had never heard of before called a "Morphic Community Center."

"MCC-San Francisco," a bored woman of indeterminate age reported in over the line.

"Yes, I understand that you help morphics connect with local services," I asked, trying to sound polite, ignoring the four new itches that had blossomed to full awareness.

God help me, I was ready to shave off my fur.

"Just a moment," she responded.

Easy for you to say, I'm the one being eaten alive.

"Yes, this is Bill, I'm an outreach coordinator. How can I help you?" he asked.

"Um, Hi Bill. This is really embarrassing, but I missed a flea treatment, and, well I'm dying here," I confessed to the sound of a muffled chuckle over the line.

"I'm sorry miss, it's just, the same thing happened to our director last week," he excused.

"It's fine, just help me please," I replied with unintended urgency.

"Sending the details to your tablet now," he informed. There was a quick vibration confirming something new had arrived.

"I think it just came in," I replied.

"Good luck, if you need us, we're here. Support group is every Wednesday at 9. I sent the address with the groomer," the line clicked.

Did he just say groomer?

Another itch sent me into a scratching overdrive.

Ok, groomer, sounds great! Tapping the number in the packet, my tablet soon connected me.

"Paula's Pretty Pets," an older woman's voice poured over the phone like rich molasses.

This was humiliating.

"Hi, I'm a morphic client and was referred to you by the resource center," I began.

"Oh, that's my other business sweetie; all morphic products, all certified, no pet stuff, guaranteed. Do you like the name Fuzz Cuts? I can't decide," she asked, her mind drifting from appointments. I had only one thing on my mind.

"I have fleas. Soonest appointment. Bonus for today." The urgent tones from my collar seemed to snap her to focus.

"Oh you poor thing; that must be simply awful, you just come right in and I'll get you worked out." Thank heavens for kind humans.

Having no recourse, and feeling like a plague bearer, I rode the Bart the thirty minutes there. Grateful it was not peak hours, being 10 in the morning, it was sparse enough that I could avoid people.

The constant scratching seemed to communicate enough for them to stay away.

In that moment, I was grateful for my harness, vague fears of animal control running through my mind like waking nightmare.

Finally, the train announced Berkley and I eagerly hopped off, stopping only to get my bearings and check my tablet for the next direction.

It maneuvered me into a neighborhood, finally coming to a house that was painted a deep royal blue, with a sign hanging off a side entrance proclaiming "Paula's Pretty Pets."

The sense of humiliation returned as I skulked up the driveway, and used my hind paw to thump the door in my approximation of a knock.

An older woman in her mid-60s popped her head out and looked left and right before noticing me.

"Oh you must be Snow, you poor dear, right this way." She ushered me in, and was suddenly all business.

"Need help with your harness?" she asked.

"Yes please," I replied. I wiggled free, and she held it with two fingers at a distance and walked off towards a room labeled "Laundry".

"Alright miss, head down the hall on your left and there's a bathroom set up for morphics. I set the product you will need on the rim." Thank God, I was grateful I could handle this myself.

I handed over my tablet and authorized payment, including a hefty tip, then moved down the hall.

It was a normal tub, with a lever faucet, easy to manipulate. Reading the directions, the product worked like a bubble bath.

That could be nice. The twitching itches returned, and I eagerly ran the hot bath, filling the dosage cap according to instructions. Using the lip of the tub as my platform to hold the cup, I carefully tipped the bottle with my forepaws, before grasping it with both and holding it under the faucet.

It fluffed up into a bubbly froth, but it had very little scent, something I was incredibly grateful for.

Sliding into the hot water, I dunked my muzzle, causing me to cough. Righting myself, sitting on my hind paws, I dunked my head a few times and then set to groom, before taking time just to soak as indicated.

'Die, you blood sucking bastards, die!' I said to myself, sans voice collar. Tiny black dots began to populate the top of the water.

Gross.

Still, the water was warming and relaxing, taking all the stress out of weary muscles; all the tightness from the stress I had been carrying seemed to slough away some, as I drifted into palpable relief.

The water seemed suddenly colder and there was a knock at the door.

"Miss?" I perked up, and set the tub to drain, reaching for my voice collar with wet paws, pulling it by its dangling band from the counter and pressing its box to my neck.

Focus... "Yeah, fell asleep. Rinsing now," I reported. There was a distant chuckle through the door. The nap was nice, it had been a night without sleep.

"Get finished up dear, just checking in," she replied.

I think I liked Paula.

A quick rinse under the pull chain shower head with surprising water pressure soon had fur feeling not just clean, but the skin underneath scrubbed; it even stung a bit, but there were no more itches.

According to the label, I was now good for six months. *Freedom.*

Nosing into a towel set on a short rack, I pushed into it and nuzzled up against it between me and the wall, working the water out of my fur as best I could with a satisfied grunt. It seemed rude to shake, though I greatly wished to. The tremor kept moving through my fur almost like a sneeze and I suppressed the instinct.

Pulling the lever-handled door, I still looked half drowned upon emerging.

"You know, you paid for it, might as well let me do a blow dry and brush," she said as my thick wet fur made me feel deeply chilled.

"That sounds grand actually," I replied, and she guided me to a room that looked like any stylist's room, except for a stainless steel worktable in the center, with a small stool next to it, instead of a chair.

"Here hop up, and I can work," she said.

The warm rivulets of current that worked their way through my fur from the dryer, soon provided ample comfort and I sagged.

It was turning out to be such a nice day.

"So are you new in the area? Moving in?" she asked, making idle conversation.

"Just here for a few months. Heading off into deep space," I replied, as if this was an everyday thing.

"Sounds adventurous, just you?" she continued.

"I was going to go with a friend, but they passed," I explained, trying to keep a safe distance from the past.

"Something like that happened to me too sweetie, My Gerald. He died on the Enterprise during the atomic apocalypse." She began to brush my fur now, and my mind interpreted it as grooming, which only relaxed me further.

"I'm sorry for your loss," I replied.

"Oh that was well over forty years ago now. It's a new world, and I have a life. I miss him every day, but I'd like to think he's proud of me. You'll make it too sweetie, you'll see." In that moment, I knew I liked her immensely.

"Thank you," I replied, feeling awkward at the sudden connection.

"So how'd you get the fleas? That sounds just awful," she said, switching subjects deftly. I could see why she was branching out from pets, she was sorely wasted there.

"You don't know the half of it; I think I got them from my hotel." The Sunset Villa Royal was best classified as a dive. Still, it was in my budget. 1500 for two months. The joys of living in San Francisco.

"You know, you're a good tipper and you seem nice. I've got a room in the back I could rent out for a couple months. Not cheap though, 1000 credits," she said.

"What's the catch?" I pushed.

"Sometimes I get chatty, and sometimes it gets busy up front, which means noise during the day," she admitted.

It was better than fleas. An image of them somehow infesting my shuttle and joining me on Centioc quickly helped me make the decision.

"I think I can work with that," I replied.

Chapter 39

My room rental had another drawback.

Long commute time, one hour each way.

It had necessitated another fifteen credit purchase. A new patch now occupied my harness, proclaiming in capital letters down my back. "DO NOT PET"

At best, it was only partially successful. Most humans do not believe rules apply to them.

The things you have to get accustomed to when you change your species.

I sighed, settling down into my seat; feeling that I had lucked out to get one, I gazed out the window.

Just a few more days of this and I'd have my license back. If everything went well, I'd be the proud owner of a shuttle by the end of the week.

No more public transportation.

This was officially cutting it close; as of this week, I had one last month on Earth, an appointment, as cargo, awaited me on the Masamune.

The special toned wail of the train against the tracks told me through blinding rivulets of sonic pain that we were nearing the spaceport, and my stop; the train was not built to consider lagomorphic ears, or anyone else's for that matter.

A dashing man in a suit walked up to the seat and sat down across from me.

"Would you like a carrot?" he asked.

"Piss off," I replied.

"You don't have to be like that," he continued, "I just wanted to tell you about Jesus."

"No thank you, and in the future, you might have better luck if its bananas, but try respect first. Seriously." The car glided to a halt and I quickly hopped off, leaving the man behind.

Last week. I reminded myself, diverting for the elevator to take me away from the passenger level.

Today's roster. Visual acuity, peripheral vision and reaction tests.

The vision test worried me; traditionally, my kind has terrible eyesight by human standard, but I felt that I saw fine. I think I still saw colors much the same as I once remembered, if a touch more muted. My peripheral vision, by human standards, was amazing.

I was a hare, but elements of my old life still functioned as legacy. It was the reason I was 94% integrated and not 97%, or 99%.

Hours of 'left paw, right paw, read the screen' followed, and my brain ached as my eyes burned by the end of the long day. Still I had passed, another box checked.

Progress.

Hopping towards home, a chime from my pouch indicated that my tablet wanted my attention. I slid off to the side of the side walk and worked it out of its hiding spot.

It was a message confirming my shuttle appointment.

A scent of a predator… a *dog,* drifted by on the wind, drawing me to look around from my distraction.

Oh shit. Someone was walking their German Shepherd and was closing in on me.

They too were distracted, walking forward while glancing down at their tablet as the dog strained the leash.

'Stupid, Snow; that was stupid letting yourself get distracted like that' The leash went taut and she got yanked forward. It was only by sheer luck that she had an actual grip that this did not devolve into chase. I launched back reflexively; the dog snarled and growled, effectively leaving me pinned between her and the fence.

"I am not food," I protested, fear driving me to full panic. She wrestled with the dog, but it struggled, trying to get at me; in a panic, I mule kicked it with both my hind paws, it yelped and slunk behind her.

"She was only trying to play," she scolded.

"Try being my size lady, call the cops, I'll wait." I replied, desperately hoping she wouldn't call my bluff.

"Bitch," she spat before tugging the leash. "Come on Coco."

She slunk off, as my heartbeat began to debate normalizing at twice the usual rhythm.

Weary from the sudden tension, I made my way towards "home".

Another day on Earth.

Chapter 40

"Just a quick trip across town." Paula begged. She was standing behind the counter at the front of her home business. I was curled up on the couch in the waiting area.

She was lying. There was no such thing as quick anywhere in the Bay Area.

"I almost got eaten by a German Shepherd today, I'm tired," I countered.

There was a sound of rustling from under the counter and a particular type of click that caused my ears to swivel with interest.

"Hay brick?" she offered.

My stomach growled.

"Can't be bought," I challenged.

"That's what they all say," she replied, and reached into her large black purse with gold accents, revealing banana chips.

"You're an evil woman," I accused.

She shrugged, "It gets results. Do we have a deal?"

"Fine," I complained, dramatically dragging myself off the couch with an exaggerated stretch and a yawn, hopping over and swiping the timothy hay brick with a grumble.

"Somebody's testy today," she observed.

"I wasn't joking about the shepherd." I insisted, as I detected the sound of car keys.

What supply store did she use that would be open at 8 PM on a Wednesday?

It didn't matter, I had food now. Dinner for a car ride didn't seem so bad.

"Are you ok? Do you need a doctor?" Paula was suddenly at my side, checking me over, doing everything but putting her hands on me.

After the last few weeks, I deeply appreciated her restraint.

"I'm ok, mule kicked the dog, got called a bitch. Such a friendly city you have here." When I was stuck in human existence, it largely had been, at worst, indifferent.

There were times now where the world seemed decidedly sinister and pointed against my direction.

Nibbling my hay brick, I lapsed into a reflective silence. It disappeared faster than I expected it to.

"You are hungry," she said.

"I'm fine," I replied. I was conserving now, to splurge for later.

A pained look crossed her face.

We made our way to the car.

The road became more windy and I began to recognize the campus.

"What are you up to? This is no store," I challenged as she came to a stop in the parking lot.

"Very good at pointing out the obvious, come and see," she said, letting my curiosity burn at me.

"I still haven't gotten my banana chips," I protested, as she opened my door.

"Like you can hop and eat them, grumpy," she scolded.

I drummed my hind paw in agitation, but nevertheless, followed along.

Wednesday, about 2100 hours... why did that sound familiar?

We entered a building that gave way to a maze of meeting rooms and classrooms. She picked one and glided in.

There were five other morphics in attendance, along with various humans, milling about in a large room.

A white tiger wearing a business suit padded up to greet me.

The support group...

"Paula, what have you done to me?" I asked.

"It's just a party. The center is throwing it as a memorial and as an outreach. Education and all that. Free meal," she explained.

"Memorial?" I asked.

"Yeah the Hope was lost a year ago, last week. There's gatherings like this all over the world today to remember them. See, this is why I did this. You don't watch the news, you don't go out. I know I'm just a nosy old woman, but I'm worried about you." She had no idea what she had done.

A year... it had been a year?

The math clicked in my head as I looked around the room.

All these people gathered around to remember Joyce and the two hundred and forty-eight ... when I had been the one to kill them.

Shame, fear, guilt, regret all crashed into me, and I found myself in motion, paws slipping across the slick tile floors as I pushed and pushed towards an exit. I needed out, needed air.

How could I have forgotten? How could I have been so busy as to let it slip my mind? The door was coming approaching up ahead, I skittered to a stop and pounded the push bar, it flew open, and I burst out, surprising two students coming up the stairs.

Streaking across the campus, the panic and the frustration of the day washed over me, as I pushed myself further and further on; my heart pounding, ears down, just running, the pain driving me on like a fire.

My hind paws soon ached, and my lungs burned. I was not built for marathons, but sprints and I had been running long by this time, longer than I was made for. My muscles burned and threatened to tear, but I just kept going.

I didn't want to stop, I wanted to run, and run, until I couldn't feel or I could see her again.

Oh God. How could I have forgotten?

I had been distracted, had been so comfortable since my emergence.

My body faltered; I missed a step and tumbled, my muzzle smacking rudely into the cold, hard ground.

Pain blossomed through my jaw and head, but there was no crack, only an aching soreness.

I just lay there, panting, on my side, staring up at the night sky, cool grass surrounding me.

A random passerby walked up to me, and upon noticing my harness, spoke.

"Are you alright ma'am?" His words startled me, wrenching my attention from the peaceful sky. I shot up. Looking around, I was in someone's front yard.

"Yeah, I'm fine," I lied, and turned, slowly making my way back towards campus after finding my bearings.

They took that as enough and continued on their way.

My tablet began to ring in its pouch on my harness. I managed to work it out. Paula was trying to get in touch, no doubt because of my quick exit.

The screen was cracked. *Perfect,* another thing I didn't need right now.

"Hi," I said after tapping the answer button, carefully.

"Snow are you ok? The way you burst out..." Her panic was evident, even in my frazzled state, swallowing air in panicked gulps, chest heaving.

"Bad memories. Not your fault. Doing better now." A three point statement detailing I was ok.

"I'd really like to listen. Please talk to me," she urged.

"I really don't know if I can," I replied. If I did, and said too much, it could put her in danger.

It could put me in danger. The admiral had not shown up at my discharge for his health.

"Well, if you ever decide you can, I'm right here," she offered.

"I'll meet you back at the car," I carefully ended the call, and put my broken tablet away.

Chapter 41

She had given me the banana chips without a word.

Otherwise, we rode home in silence.

Guilt seemed to eat at her, as the next two days wore on, and I got my provisional license back, enough to buy the shuttle this weekend and take my final test on Monday.

Still, I was worried about Paula; she had become a helicopter person. Distant, but always present at the edges. Tormented.

It was Friday, late in the evening; my appointment to view the shuttle at the space port was tomorrow and Paula flitted by nervously, wanting to "clean".

Clean was code for "check up on me" after the events of Wednesday.

I drew out my tablet, and held it out to her.

"Take mine, and take yours, leave them in the front room near the counter, then come back here and shut the door," I ordered and she eyed me concernedly.

"What is it you are up to?" she asked.

"I'll tell you in a minute, but this has to stop," I admitted, and the guilty look on her face intensified.

"Snow, I'm sorry," she said.

"It's fine, just please, do as I ask," I demanded, and she complied without a further word.

A few minutes later, she was standing there, in front of the door with it shut behind her.

"So what's this all about?" she asked.

"I was on the Danube, when the Hope died. Joyce Coswell was my best friend," I related in rapid fire bursts, speaking more in that moment about what had happened then I had to anyone else before.

"What happened?" she pushed for more information.

"I can't say anymore. Suffice it to say, I left the service, and it's the reason I'm going to Centioc," I explained.

"The tablets are in the other room, just like you asked. No one can hear us, I know you're concerned, but there's more to it than that." Her eyes focused on me, I could feel their intensity. My chest heaved, as I relived it all over again.

"I can't say too much more, but I was the astrogator... Was forced to leave them behind. Please don't ask me anymore, I don't want to talk about it anymore. Don't want to think about how I... killed her." My voice, even through my collar, shook; my heart raced, and I wanted to swoon, or run, or die, whichever got me the fastest away from the awful memories.

"I had no idea." The awareness dawned across her face.

"Oh God Snow, I'm so sorry I did that to you; I just wanted you to make a few friends," she explained.

"Paula, I don't hate you, you're one of the kindest humans I've met post shift, proof that there's hope for the species," I praised, fully meaning it.

She blushed. "I don't know if I'd go that far."

"I would, it's a cast of thousands out there, but you stand out," I continued.

"Oh, it's not that bad," she scolded.

"It's not good and bad. People seem to value the pre-eminence of their own viewpoints over others. It makes everything twisted, but I'm learning something. In a way, it's all valid? I'm a hare, you're a human; Joyce was an otter, a feral like me. She had the same challenges, ran into bad people, but you know how she treated it?" Her memory burned like a bright blue star in my mind.

"How?" She asked.

311

"Games. It was all joy for Joyce, even the ugly parts. Paula, I woke up in the tank and felt more alive and complete then I had my entire life, but at the end of the day, it was still me living the life. A new me, hopefully better than the old, but I continued. My bias continues, my viewpoint continues and so does everyone else's. It starts to go wrong, and get ugly when people think theirs is the only one that matters." The words were imperfect, the idea half formed, but I was coming to something.

Paula approached and sat down on the bed, next to the chair I was currently perched in; she reached out her hand, and then stopped, waiting for confirmation. I nodded.

She gently stroked my ears, eliciting a flutter from my left hind paw.

"You know, you don't have to leave. Stick around a while, keep an old woman company," Paula offered.

"It's not that easy. I made deals, agreements with people that will see that I keep them. There was a cost for my freedom, Paula, and I'm still paying it. I'm going to be paying it for the rest of my life. That's my duty, and that's my path. Even this conversation is taking a risk, a big one. Hence my concern about the tablets." The conviction was firm within me. Joyce's last words echoed, my black act damming me by my own conscience, yet distantly now.

Agreements worked with infernal powers were extracting their consequences to full and devastating effect.

Paula rose, and set down a hay brick on the table; they were becoming a regular feature. I'd find bundles of them waiting when I got home from re-certification every day.

She cared. The idea rocketed through me, bringing with it a warmth, a sense of belonging, comfort, as if pieces of my spirit, numbed by experience were slowly responding again from a long, death-like sleep.

My joy was always short lived; memories of Joyce rose in counterpoint, the panicked noises from the final transmission. The inescapable reality that the last person I truly cared about, I had murdered with my cowardice.

The emotions screaming within me; I winced, and dipped my muzzle down, hopping to the bed, curling around her otter plush.

"Thank you for trusting me. I promise you, I'll never utter a word of this to another soul," Paula announced, stroking me a few more times along my ears before leaving me to my grief.

Chapter 42

The Scout-89 set upon a private shuttle pad in San Francisco International Space Port.

Most likely, it deserved to be in a museum.

It was old, from 2040, nine years before I was born, and clearly showing its age. Constructed by rivet and outdated welding techniques, you could see light dustings of rust in its thick, layered hull at the seams. She was a relic of another time.

"She's ancient, but has been retrofitted twice and refueled recently, containing a gen-3 fusion reactor onboard. Those are rare. Can't kill them, they last forever," a UEA quartermaster explained, focused only on his mission of salesmanship. He was in his 40s, and was wearing a flight suit, holding a digital clipboard.

My ears perked at the mention of recent refueling, but the ship itself was fascinating; it showed how much had changed.

I had read about these in high school. These ships patrolled out in three months arcs and were crewed by two man teams at the very beginnings of human stellar exploration, a time when there was little support, and little help.

"It has four layers of hull?" I commented, in no way an engineer.

"Oh yeah, they never trusted anything back in those days. Everything in this ship is redundant. You should meet my grandad, talks about this stuff all the time," he said with a smile, trying to be affable.

My curiosity was peaked. "Was he a pilot?"

"Nah, mechanic, worked out of the Watchtowers out near Saturn. That's where these babies deployed from," he said, proudly sharing his family history.

Everyone knew about the Watchtowers, the initial defensive perimeter. Just after the atomic apocalypse in 2031, the Far Horizon Project, a drone with the first near light drive prototype, crossed the boundaries of the outer solar system and entered interstellar space.

The world held its breath as it registered an external detonation before falling silent, its feed abruptly cut.

There, on the edge of their own created annihilation, a new fear was sown into humanity, that they were not alone and vulnerable in the night.

In a second fiery moment, the world had changed again, uniting under the banner of the UEA against potentially greater threats lurking just beyond the veil of the solar system.

Fourteen years later, the Hammerhead was commissioned, the first human space-based warship; these shuttles bridged the gap in time and were part of the initial defense.

"So what do you think?" he asked, snapping me out of my reflection. He was eager, if not the greatest salesman.

"I think I like it," I replied, bounding up the ramp. The cabin was one large room, rows of toggle switches lined panels, and keypads with LED lights blinked from their perch; there were very few touchscreens or anything fancy. Many of the keypads seemed strangely polished, their numbering chipped and faded from millions of moments of contact with human hands.

"Well, then, how about we just sit down in my office, and discuss the terms of sale?" he replied with a grin.

It really wasn't like I had any other choice. "Ok, buddy," I replied.

Three hours and 85,000 credits later, I had a new home, and could almost fly it.

With that done, it was time for stage two. I had a flight test on Tuesday, and had to get it retrofitted before then.

No pressure.

Still, the analog nature, and mechanical construction of the shuttle made that much easier. It was largely set up, and a few aftermarket strap-ins and a longer chain for the shower would essentially have it configured to work with my dexterity.

Nonetheless, there were some things that I had to have professionally done, but for now, I just needed to be able to fly it.

Now, if I could just get the package open....

Furred paws do not do well on plastic packaging. Its inner contents contained a type of sling that fit over the pilot's joystick. It would compress my paw to the yoke, and relieve my need to grip it as hard, providing me with better contact to the essential control device of the ship.

Open... you damn thing... My fingers, such as they were, kept slipping.

It met its match when it met my teeth. Strong incisors, built for the destruction of twigs, sticks and stalks proved an ample match for plastic blister packaging.

Someone in product design was definitely getting their chuckles out of this.

Fumbling with it, getting it slid over the stick, it took a few more minutes of adjustment, but I was able to slide my paw into it... It felt good, and I was feeling less worried about killing myself, or the instructor due to dexterity issues.

Generally, thundering in, in a fiery heap, is looked upon poorly in proficiency evaluations. Go figure.

Heavy boots thudded up the ramp, causing my ears to swivel instinctively towards their direction, as I added what I could to the ship, to make its operation more streamlined.

"You need to clear this pad, this shuttle's been sold," a security officer barked gruffly, his frame silhouetted against the bright light streaming in from outside, in stark contrast with the lamps of the cabin.

"Just a moment. Working on that presently," I responded, distracted in the pilot's seat, working out the control scheme.

Com to the left side, guidance on the right, diagnostics center ahead of stick...

All standard. The jutting silver toggle switches were novel. No shiny buttons.

"You got fifteen minutes or we're moving it for ya, long ears," he reported, with a heavy turn before thudding down the ramp just as quickly.

Punching a few commands into a keypad, the shuttle connected to the data server at the spaceport; on an upper-left monitor, a map of the terminal appeared.

It was just a quick trip to long-term parking. This was simple business, and did not even require a radio into ground control.

I kept reminding myself of that fact as I flipped its switches, and entered commands. With a shaking rumble, it came to life, a high pitched whine seemed to grow in intensity and pitch in the back as the reactor spun up, before abruptly falling silent.

No angels yet, now to see if I could move the thing.

Flipping the switch for the ramp, it raised, and I prepared for my first flight as a lagomorphic pilot.

Nervousness ate at the edges of my resolve, and my paw trembled as I engaged its taxi mode. The craft leapt up off the pad, and hovered steadily in the air.

Progress...

The sling hurt my paw slightly, needed adjustment, but there was no time or opportunity to do that on the fly; for now, I had to get it across the terminal, and onto its new pad. That would be enough for the day.

It was a ten minute trip, but for me it took half an hour. Moving slow, watching, hyper-vigilant. I was exhausted by the time I came to rest at shuttle pad C, but I was here, and I was done, ready for my flight test.

Sliding my aching paw out of the sling, I collapsed heavily down into the pilot's seat.

Mayhem managed, I finally had time to think. Hopping down from the chair, I regarded my new world.

This was home now. Sure, I was staying with Paula until I deployed on the sixteenth next month, but this was going to be my home.

Centioc... alone. Was I really going to do this?

The 85,000 credits missing from my bank account certainly seemed to indicate in that direction, not to mention the admiral at my discharge from the hospital.

Like it or not, this was my life now.

Strange feelings rumbled through me as the conviction settled home. This was *mine*, and that meant something.

Hopping around through the new space, nosing through cabinets, I found tiny relics of its life, running many crews, performing many duties. A bit of graffiti, hidden behind a shelf reported that Jackson was there in '42.

I wondered where he was now, and if he still remembered the 89.

Poking around, I found a few other memorials and mementos, relics of months in deep space with little to do, and felt a growing kinship with my new craft.

Just like me, she was haunted by old ghosts. We made a good pair.

An instinct seized me; without a thought, I leaned up on my hind paws and ran my lower jaw along a beam above the lower bunk. Chinning. Making it my own.

The action, only tied me further to this new space, making me feel more connected to it.

Yes, I think I liked her, which was good, because like it or not, we were going to be together for a long time.

Chapter 43

My stomach was doing somersaults, as I nibbled down a hay brick. The overpowering aroma of coffee, along with sweet perfume competed, dominating any other smell, as Paula sat across from me, watching in silence.

"Today is the big day, hmm?" she asked, taking a sip.

"Yep, after this, the month is mine until I head up to my ride to Centioc," I reported. The time had melted by in a blur; Joyce had been gone for over a year, and so much had changed in that time. There was a feeling of distance to John, and my old life, even what I had done. Everything that had happened in the meantime filled up too much space, had pushed things out to the horizon.

Still, at night especially, when everything got quiet, I could hear her last words to me echoing like a distant ghost. Reminding me of the black stains upon my soul.

Don't let this kill you, don't let this stop you. Remember me. I love you...

As much as those words had become an agony, they had also been my salvation. They were the only reason I had persisted through the first, long months following the event, and now, they urged me on, back towards the stars, even though I had the beginnings of a new life here.

It was a false spring; as much as I had found friendship in Paula, and something nearing a home in my tiny back room, my future was on Centioc One. Whether I wanted to go or not, was immaterial. Some choices are made for you.

"It sounds so lonely, what you're doing. What happens if you need help? What happens if something goes wrong?" Her concern was touching, Paula gave me reasons to hope.

"Manage as I best I can. I told you, I made promises, but it's more than that. Call it fate, call it destiny. Something is pulling me out there. Some of it, I know is my Ghosts, the promises I feel I have to keep, but there's something more there. My fate is on that planet, not this one." It hardly made sense to me, which made it even harder to explain.

"It sounds lonely." She fired another salvo in mock debate, as she took another long pull off her coffee.

"Hares are solitary creatures. I'll be fine," I excused, as my tablet vibrated.

"You better get moving," she intoned, knowing just as much as I that it was my signal to hop down to the BART station.

"I should, wish me luck," I replied, taking the time to stretch and pop my back.

Paula rose and petted back my ears, then offered me another hay brick. I quickly scarfed it down.

"Good luck. If you run into any problems, just call, I'll be there," she reminded, brooding like a mother hen.

"Will do," I turned and she opened the door; I darted out, and hopped at rapid pace all the way down the three blocks to the BART station. Speed was my ally, especially in the human world.

Come to think of it, it was not so different for hares in the wild either.

It was an uneventful ride. The normal parade of human ignorance, curiosity and apathy, and I soon found myself back at long term parking, the instructor waiting outside of the shuttle.

"Miss Dawkins, right on time. I'm Jeremy Potter, let's get this out of the way," he announced, in neutral tones. It felt refreshing that, for the moment, he considered me to be nothing more than a prospective pilot, saying nothing about my form, and showing no reaction to it.

"Works for me," I replied, and began a thorough check, starting with a walk around, looking for issues with my craft, as he watched from a distance with an inscrutable look upon his face, taking the time to tap at his large tablet that he carried, or enter data into it. After fifteen minutes of largely perfunctory tests, we were ready to board.

"Ok, strap in, seat belts," I called out, which earned a few more taps of his tablet.

More, largely unnecessary, checks.

Reactor Fuel Level... Check

Cabin Pressurization... Check

Life Support... Check

Lighting... Check

Guidance and Coms... Check

I ran her through every diagnostic check I could think of; the list went on and on, as he worked himself down into his seat, bored out of his mind. Me, I was on the edge of terror.

After a full half hour of diagnostics, and function tests, I finally broke the silence apart from my call outs.

"We are board green and ready for flight, all systems report stable. Ready to move to flight test on your order." I slipped back into old patterns from the military, trusting them to guide me through.

"Well, you certainly are thorough," he commented; it was the first time he had said anything that didn't make him sound like a robot.

"Can't afford not to be, especially not today," I replied in near desperate tones.

"Relax, all I care about is that you don't kill anyone, me included. So far, you are passing with flying colors. Let's go through the ground control clearances, make a quick loop into orbit and you'll be all done," he smiled, loosening up some.

It felt good to know that at least he was impartial. It buffeted me; I knew I could still fly, even if the butterflies in my stomach were having a thrash concert complete with mosh pit.

I flipped up the com switch.

"Ground Control," came a dispassionate voice from over the speaker.

"This is Snow Dawkins, aboard the Scout-89, requesting clearance for an orbital loop for mandatory evaluation and testing," I reported, following protocol to the letter.

"I have you, transponder is pinging, clearance granted. Safe flight and good luck miss," came the reply from the controller.

The butterflies seemed to triple in number, and, no longer content with their concert, decided to go for a quick, and bloody war, but still, I held by falling into the rigmarole of routine that had carried me through years in the service.

"If you're ready, let's get underway," I reported, as Mr. Potter nodded, slipping back into his detached ease.

I worked my paw into the sleeve that held my paw to the yoke, and flipped a few switches. The 89 leapt up into the air, and I very gently began my ascent up into the heavens, setting course and guidance. It took thirty minutes, we ascended into orbit and then I guided us back down, landing again safely on the pad.

Potter sighed, and tapped a few more entries into his device. "Congratulations miss, you passed. You are a safe and sane pilot, better than many I've tested and passed."

"Thank you," I replied and relaxed, as I lowered the ramp.

Every hurdle in front of me, I had handled. Every challenge was done. With just a few weeks remaining, there was no longer anything to stop me from leaving.

That thought hung in the air, like heavy storm clouds. Just like that, my pilgrimage was over, and now, there was only the fruits of my labor to collect.

A lifetime alone, mourning the people I had ended with my cowardice.

In that moment, I truly did not want to go, but it mattered little. With a heavy heart, I shut down the shuttle, and began to make my way back towards my temporary home.

Chapter 44

The month melted by in a blur, but all things come to an end.

That was one lesson, I had firmly learned.

San Francisco International Spaceport. Private shuttle parking. My old rust bucket, quickly retrofitted and crammed full of food, now waiting, with its ramp down.

My last day on Earth.

The feelings competed with my memories of Joyce, the familiar pattern of their interruptions a normal part of my life. It was as if they had become a filter that engaged at will, shaping my view of my world.

Now, it was my turn to wonder if I would ever return, and of what awaited me.

The excitement wasn't there. I was going to be alone. It would be quiet, but it's what I had wanted. Time away. Distance from everything that had ever made me damn them.

"I don't want you to go." Paula was a blubbering mess, wiping tears from her eyes unsuccessfully with a makeup stained tissue.

"I have to, I'm sorry. Still, I will never forget you or your kindness. You saved me Paula, showed me some people are still good. I'll never be able to thank you enough for that."

An agonized yelp escaped as she went down on one knee and hugged me without preamble, crushing me against her softer, yet larger frame.

"You are a good sweet bunny. You remember to eat now." She stroked my ears affectionately.

"Good Luck, and thank you again." I hopped aboard and began flipping switches, sliding my paw into the modified sling that let me easily manipulate the joystick.

Tilting to my left, I flipped up the metal switch for radio access.

"This is Scout-89, requesting orbital exit arc towards the Masamune, transmitting credentials."

More switches to flip. A light illuminated over a card slot, where a tiny chip contained the flight path data I had entered. Everything in this old bucket was manual, from a different era of space travel long before man was comfortable out there.

Paula waved as the ramp drew to a close.

"Flight path approved Scout-89, safe flight," Ground Control confirmed.

With a rumbling shake, the shuttle went through its startup and began to ascend from the pad. Rising into the sky soon revealed the familiar back drop of space. The near eternal theater of stars, waiting always just beyond the blue veil of Earth's sky.

An hour passed, then I came upon the Masamune spinning in space. With minimal greeting, and no reception, I made my way forward, matching her rotation. I was cargo, I reminded myself, as I glided to a halt in the shuttle bay and then was largely forgotten.

Seven months ticked by in that tiny space. The days bled into one another as I kept myself busy with equations, maneuvers and binge consumption of media. There were no visitors. Just me. Just the silence I had earned.

While I was within range, I had kept in touch with Paula, but the old radios lost their reach after the first jump.

My world faded, became small and quiet. With no need for my harness or collar, I packed them away in my old foot locker, containing the relics of my former life.

Routine, for months the same routine, of wake up, busy myself until sleep. Finally, a day came where I had to fish my collar out of the box to work with ops, as they dropped me off just outside the Gate, my last month drifting slowly, half the time accelerating, half the time decelerating.

Hurry up and wait.

Finally, after an eternity of stars, a blue-green planet appeared in the window of the shuttle, complete with a strange asteroid moon, irregularly shaped, floating in the spectral night.

Pulling up the data for the colony, there were two large clearings; I selected the smaller of the two, and began my descent to my new home.

Landing, the ramp lowered on my new home. By that time, I was fully accustomed to the silence. Centioc had wind though, and weather. Cycles of sunrise and sunset. They were welcome changes, after months in isolation. Otherwise, it was calm, and peaceful. I was the first resident of the world that did not have roots.

I explored. Happy to be free of my confines. The first month passed quickly. I made daily runs from my clearing, to the colony site. Then, the second month drifted by, followed by another.

I stopped keeping track. I stopped doing a lot of things. Memories of that dream, just a scant few days before my tanking, became my reality. I spent my days, watching, from the top of the ramp, or under my shuttle, as the meadow drifted by, as we quietly orbited the star.

Spring, to summer then winter and back again. Sometimes it rained, sometimes it snowed; the wind blew, and the plants went about their cycles, but little else changed.

I quietly waited, and watched, content to be a forgotten relic, of a life that could have been, on a distant world, deep in space, until even that faded.

By the time I realized I was slipping towards feralism, maybe two or three years in, I hardly cared. I had my nest of blankets, I had my clearing, everything I needed. Until, one day, even words started to get strange.

Don't let this kill you, don't let this stop you. Remember me...

The words echoed, their meaning mostly lost, but their impact still, somehow brought emotion, and connection. I nosed into the otter plush that stayed with me in my nest of blankets under the table. An explosion of scents, my own, mixed with hers, brought her to the forefront of my fading mind.

Fish friend. I could never forget her, even while I forgot everything else. A heaviness pulled me down. For now it was time to sleep.

The story continues in Book 2 of The Farthest Star series: *Exile's Return.*

From the author...

Thank you for reading Dawnbreak! If this story connected I'd like to ask you the favor of rating and reviewing it on Amazon. For independent authors like myself, four and five star reviews are more valuable than gold.

Studio Prey rose from the ashes in 2017 with a mission of producing stories that change you. If you'd like to know more, please visit us at https://www.studioprey.com/. There you will find the latest updates on new content, opportunities for early access to upcoming works vis-à-vis the Final Draft Club, and the novelette Gateways, which surrounds the Promethean moment of the signing of the Treaty of Gates.

Stop by if you can, we'll keep a place by the fire open, just for you.

Warm Regards,

Rebecca Mickley

About Rebecca Mickley

I grew up in the middle of a cotton field with a library card. It was my ticket to adventures beyond the world I knew and experienced day to day. I grew and changed, eventually leaving that place, but the stories I gathered along the way shaped my perspective, and changed me. Now I seek to do the same for my readers.

I invite you to take up a chair by the fire, and listen as I spin my tales. I cannot always promise you a happy ending, but I can promise you an experience that you will never forget.

Other Titles By Rebecca Mickley

The Farthest Star Series

Available on StudioPrey.com
Gateways – Book 0.5 (Only available on StudioPrey.com)
Dawnbreak – Book 1
Exile's Return – Book 2
Rise of the Forgotten – Book 3
The Farthest Star – Book 4
Sins of the Solar Republic – Book 5
Electronic Souls – Book 6
Captain Tosk – Book 7
Starfall – Book 8
Angels of Our Yesterday – Book 9
Demons of Our Tomorrow – Book 10

The Nightmare God Series

Hillsong Chronicles Series

(Bonus)
Exile's Return

The Farthest Star Series – Book 2

Chapter 1

// NEURAL ACTIVITY DETECTED, INITIATING LOG //

Fear, panic, the noise, the smell! Big Predator! Something was here. Run, flee, have to get away!

I dashed for my home, the tiny nest in the big cave. Streaking past the open door, I landed safe, happy in my home. It would surely never find me here.

I could hear it. It was coming closer. It was making strange noises. Something seemed familiar about this noise. I heard it again, "HELLO, LIEUTENANT! Are you here? HELLLO?"

Scary noise, very loud, it must not be afraid of anything. Is it hungry? Does it want to eat me?

Fear pushed me back into the dark back corner of the nest, its comforting smells doing nothing for me. Suddenly, a dim spark in the back of my mind began to glow, like an ember catching dry grass.

There was something, something special about that noise it was making. That smell, it was so familiar. Fear was goading me to run, but... but... I had to remember. Something... so important. I had to.

Like lightning, my eyes snapped open. *Shit, what happened?* I shook my head trying to take stock while my instincts prodded me to hide, to run. *Wait, wait, I have to get a grip. Calm down, calm down. Bring your instincts under control.*

I hit a computer panel and gasped. The display was covered in dust, the screen flickering with the burden of age. Its message was as shocking as it was brief. It read: *Your last log on was over 3 years ago.*

My eyes were wide with horror, the realization slowly dawning on me. The terrible reality, three years, lost to feral. Three years without thought or memory.

"HELLO!" The voice was close now, snapping me out of my sudden reflection. I had to think about what to do. Thinking was like pushing through a cold gel, concepts forming under the ice of years of lack of use.

I sneezed as I shook, and saw some dust fly up off the console. The room looked like a relic, forgotten and abandoned. A spot under the table held a nest of blankets. Somewhere, something inside me thought *"safe."* What the hell had happened? I came here to escape, not lose myself.

I heard a twig snap, and suddenly I skittered towards the door. Damn, they were getting close. Fragments of memory came floating back to me. How easy it was to relax, and let the animal take control. How seductive, how terribly liberating it had been, just to let… it… *slip*…

No, dammit! Not now. Plenty of time to deal with my departure from reality later. *Shit, I'm running out of time. Think Snow, dammit, what do you need? Voice collar! That's right!* A dark part of my mind wondered if I could still use it. Knocking dust off of old boxes I finally came across it, purple with a morphic identifier tag. I held the two ends and counted to five, but it failed to respond. The batteries were dead. Frustrated, I dropped it, just as I heard steps coming up the way.

I hit the switch, that had been hastily bolted to the frame at my level, allowing the door to slide open before he could knock, every instinct telling me it was a stupid move, as I stared up at him. He towered over me, sending an involuntary spasm of fear through my body that made my fur stand on end. Fear reached up from the darkness and threatened to paralyze me, but my reason was still driving. I began making sign only to be unceremoniously interrupted by this male with choking cologne. At least there didn't seem to be any more of them. He motioned to me and spoke rapidly.

"Wait, wait just a minute." He fumbled in a pack on his right side, various bits falling out as he rapidly searched it. Finally he gave a satisfied "Aha!" as he pulled out a voice collar.

He really was tall, even for a human, about 1.88 meters, with black hair and green eyes. He wore a uniform, much like the one I had worn aboard the Danube when I was in the service. His boots were polished to a high shine. His scent, his real one, was a mystery because of that god-awful cologne he was wearing.

I snatched the collar from his hand and pressed it to my neck. It activated, locking itself around my neck of its own accord and handshaking with the nanites inside my bloodstream. Concentrating, I tried to speak.

Nothing came at first, but unused pathways and micro machinery slowly ground to life. The effort was almost painful, but it was getting easier to take control. It was coming back to me, and with stuttering halts I began to speak.

"Wa...wa..." I stuttered, trying to make the words form in my mind, "What... reason... came...?"

I began to pant, exhausted with the mental effort it took to use it. As the man spoke my heart was still pounding, but slowly anger was taking the place of the fear I felt. This man was an intruder; he had barged into my home unwelcomed. This would not go unanswered.

"Lt. Dawkins, I came here to seek your help. We have a matter that could use your attention."

"Don't... Care... Leave! Shoo! Bad... smelly... thing!" I spat, cursing myself for being so out of practice. Something told me the words I had just used would not be the most effective, but inside I still felt very scrambled.

"Lieutenant, do I need to remind you that you are subject to involuntary recall at any time per your initial service agreement?" He crossed his arms, standing implacable.

"No, no, no! Go away, leave, leave!" Inside my mind, part of me thought I had gone completely insane staring this thing down, but I held on.

"Lieutenant? Are you OK?" he asked, looking down at me, sounding concerned, though whether for me or for his mission was unclear. "Your speech is barely coherent. Look, we have a doctor on the ship. We will get you checked out, then we can go over the details."

I shook my head rapidly. "No need you help! Long time... No talk. Talk, making noise. Shoo! Go away." Slowly words were coming back, patterns, making my speech more useful. I put my forepaws on my head and cursed my lazy brain. "I... Fine... is... coming back... Patience... long... time, no talk... Rusty."

"OK, I can wait," he said. "I can't leave here without you anyway."

We'll see about that, I thought. I wasn't about to go back with him or anyone else. This was my home, and I wasn't going to leave it. Neither the UEA nor Earth Central had any authority here. Centioc One was an unclaimed, mostly uncharted world. It was the main reason why I had come.

There was no way they could get to me here. Or so I had thought.

"Piss... off! Seven years, long time, you have no claim." I slammed down a paw for emphasis, the words coming easier now as my nanites got used to transmitting my thoughts again.

I watched him closely. In truth, my instincts wouldn't let me look away. He muttered something about "doing it the hard way" and gave a sigh. I cocked my head; he was obviously not used to dealing with a morphic with sharp hearing.

"It seems anger helps your speech, lil' bunny. Are the words coming easier now?" He was taunting me. I stared at him in disbelief. Wasn't he just trying to get me medical help? My mind still wasn't working right and couldn't decipher the sudden shift in his mood. "Under the Emergency Recall Act, we have the authority to reactivate you. Thanks to your conversion you are still healthy, young, viable and ready for a mission. Now, are you coming peacefully or do we have to use force? I'm willing to take a bet as to how far you can get before I drop you with my pistol. Don't worry, it's only on stun." The bastard seemed to be enjoying this. He smiled at me the way a kid smiled before he ripped the wings off a fly.

"Piss on your damn act. This isn't Earth, nor is it an aligned world. For all intents and purposes it is uninhabited. Your law has no effect." I was making a quick recovery, and I inwardly thanked the gods of Nano Augmentation.

342

"Didn't you see the news?" The bastard was toying with me at this point. I looked up sourly at him as he continued to speak. "As of this morning this is an Earth-aligned world. We officially laid claim."

An Earth-aligned world? Whatever was going on was bad enough that they were willing to claim this entire backwater planet for the force of law. I suppose it didn't matter to them. Theirs or not, they could do what they wanted at will anyway. I had learned at least that much in my years of service to these bastards.

I looked up, crestfallen, beginning to feel the noose tighten. This was serious, I could not find any way out, and that voice in my head telling me to run was sounding more and more tempting. I felt trapped and scared. My thinking was still muddled. I was trying to make sense of this, but my mind kept flashing to a feeling of being trapped, being up against a wall, cornered. My heart was beating sickeningly fast, and I had to will myself to keep calm and not to run.

Sighing, feeling more and more defeated the longer this went on, I asked, "What do you want me to do?"

"Lieutenant, we want you to talk to the Mendians for us. We think your unique position will be valuable."

"I haven't spoken to anyone in years. Why would you even want me? What's so unique about my position? I was just an astrogator!"

"All I know is that they asked for you," he said quietly.

"Asked, for... me? Not possible! You must be joking..."

"Afraid not, and the rub of it is, we don't know why either. We need you to come with us, to help us figure it out."

"Well, what happens if I refuse?" I asked defiantly. "I'm not exactly up to helping your sort; what are you going to do if I just refuse to go along?"

"Trust me, you don't want to do that," he replied flatly. "Look, I don't want to be anymore nasty than I have been already."

"Nasty? Is that what you call it? Coming to someone's planet and dragging them off in chains! What happens if I refuse?" I demanded again. The anger flowed through the voice collar and I saw him take a step back. For all of his bravado he did not seem to be enjoying this.

"If you refuse you will be stunned, and transported Earthside where you will be tried for desertion and treason. You will get life imprisonment or worse, and you will never see a scrap of green again; we will make sure of it. You can either go easy, or say goodbye to your quiet little sanctuary." He almost snarled it out. "The choice is yours, go easy, or go hard. Either way you are leaving today. I'm sorry, but that is the message I was told to deliver. Those are my orders." Something in his eyes flashed. It almost looked like regret, but everything about him showed the work and the discipline of a professional soldier. It seemed obvious that for him, this was just business.

He unsheathed his pistol, a sleek model of black and chrome, with a green energy bar on its left side. He checked the setting and aimed it right at me. I felt my blood run cold and the rage build within me.

"You know it's sons of bitches like you that were the reason I left in the first place! I've had a gun pointed at me before, but I suppose you know that. Does that gun make you feel big, mister?

"You may address me as Lieutenant Commander Charles Stevens. Are you coming or not?" he said flatly, my bravado having no effect.

I looked at the pistol menacingly. At that moment I hated him. Memories flashing through my mind, of that fateful day on the Danube. I scanned around, turning slightly, but he aimed more intently and said, "That is not advisable. I can make this easy for you. I know you aren't dumb. It's obvious. You have to have some kind of brain to do all that math for astrogation. Come with me peacefully, help us work this out, and you can come back. In and out, I swear. You have my word as an officer."

I felt trapped. Panic threatened to seize me. The instincts were so loud to run, it was agonizing beating them down, but no, I couldn't. *Couldn't I?* No! He had me dead to rights. The only way out was to cooperate, as odious a proposition as it was to do so. I had to play nice.

"Well, Lieutenant Commander, given my options, I suppose I have no choice. Give me a few minutes to pack. By the way, when you note this in your log, I expect you to document that this is under protest and against my will."

"Certainly, Lieutenant, as long as you're coming, I don't care if you want me to document that you're a pink unicorn. I will do everything I can to make this as pleasant as possible for you."

I was heartbroken, but I couldn't let them see it, I wouldn't give them the satisfaction. As he left, I kept my composure until I let the doors slide closed. God dammit, this was a nightmare!

I remembered back to eight years ago, the first day out of the clinic. I had felt more free in that moment then at any other in my life. I ran my paws through the cool black dirt, and tasted my first sprigs of fresh grass and reveled in the joy of being a new creature, with a new life. I had sold my house and cashed out my pension to afford this shuttle and my passage out to Centioc One. I looked around at the dust-covered relics of a life that I had almost completely abandoned three years ago. Something deep within me still saw all this as valuable. After all, my nest was still right there, under the table, the blankets bearing a familiar shape. I stood in my sanctuary, my last refuge from humanity, and their hatred, greed, and violence. I had run beyond the stars to escape them, but I had

346

not run far enough. Now they were going to drag me back, to serve them again.

I ran my paws over my old foot locker, something that had been with me since Basic and followed me home after my honorable discharge. Like everything else in my quarters, it was covered in dust. I kicked up a cloud of the choking stuff and sneezed again. Cleaning it off, I could see my old name in bright yellow letters. It read *Dawkins, J. SN# 488-9292-6516.* I had buried my old life and my past in this box, and now I was digging it up again. Struggling, I suppressed the old memories, determined not to relive the past.

Ferreting out my harness, I slipped it on, clipped it and then pulled with my teeth to cinch it home. Being a snowshoe hare, as much as I am at least, you have to learn how to deal with limitations in dexterity. The lower one gave me less trouble, and I stretched and tried to adjust to the unfamiliar restriction. I slid off the voice collar that the captain had given me and took its power module, sliding it into the purple collar that held my service tags and my identity disk. Checking to see that I had everything, I dusted my paws a couple of times and began to head for the door.

I caught my tiny mirror on the way out. How long had it been since I last looked? My fur was un-groomed and tussled, I looked like a wild animal, and I realized I had been living as one for a while now. Not much about me was different, aside from my wild appearance, still about 1.2 meters tall if you counted my ears. I'd really stand out among my feral cousins, since I was almost three times their size. I smoothed down my fur, self-conscious, and wiggled my stubby, almost useless paw-like fingers through my fur. I was about as non-morphic as they came, but rudimentary thumbs were useful even though mine still heavily limited me; I often ended up using my muzzle.

I looked back from my mirror, and towards the door. It shook me out of my reflection and refocused me on my hate. God, I hated them, I didn't want to go with them, but he had outlined it well, I had little choice, I could choose a little time now or the rest of my existence. It was logical but it didn't stop hate from welling back up within my soul. I could feel my forepaws trembling, and *dammit* I didn't want to go quietly, but it was the only way, the only way I could get back here was to do their bidding. I sighed, letting old habits and old memories take over and teach me how to be. There was so much different now, and so much still the same.

I thought back to the Lt. Commander, and what he had said. Aside from leaving, it didn't sound so bad. They wanted me to talk to the Mendians, and then I could come back, no problems. Now, I didn't trust them to really keep their word, but if all they needed me for was to talk, maybe it would be as easy as it seemed. Something inside told me he was sincere when he talked about making it easy for me. If I was stuck, I was stuck. I just had to press on, get it done and get back home. Just a short mission, surely I could handle that.

The story continues in Book 2 of The Farthest Star series:
Exile's Return

Made in the USA
Middletown, DE
03 June 2023

31981933R00208